Egg and Me

David Grant

Non-fiction section by Christopher Edge

www.pearsonschoolsandfecolleges.co.uk

✓ Free online support
✓ Useful weblinks
✓ 24 hour online ordering

0845 630 33 33

Part of Pearson

Heinemann is an imprint of Pearson Education Limited, Edinburgh Gate, Harlow, Essex, CM20 2JE.

www.pearsonschoolsandfecolleges.co.uk

Heinemann is a registered trademark of Pearson Education Limited

Text © David Grant 2011
Non-fiction text © Christopher Edge
Cover design by Wooden Ark Studio
Typeset by Kamae Design
Cover photo © Duncan Walker/istockphoto

The rights of David Grant and Christopher Edge to be identified as authors of this work have been asserted by them in accordance with the Copyright, Designs and Patents Act 1988.

First published 2011

14 13 12 11 10
10 9 8 7 6 5 4 3 2 1

British Library Cataloguing in Publication Data
A catalogue record for this book is available from the British Library

ISBN 978 0 435 04603 3

Printed at Henry Ling, UK

Acknowledgements

We would like to thank the following schools and students for their invaluable help in the development and trialling of this book:

Belper School, Derbyshire: Wayne Bailey, Izaak Devine, Harry Everley, Sam Mart, Joseph Turner, Thomas Tween, Andrew Winfield.

Holyhead School, Birmingham: Ajay Sivia, Dashaun Ming-Stanford, Hassan Ibrahim, Ikram Hussain, Ayob Mahmood, Uwais Mahmood.

Contents

Chapter 1, A Door   1

Chapter 2, Up the Down Stairs   3

Chapter 3, Eg   15

Chapter 4, More Doors, More Stairs   25

Chapter 5, The Outside World   32

Chapter 6, Daylight Robbery   39

Chapter 7, The Worst   46

Chapter 8, The Throne   57

Chapter 9, The Assembly   66

Chapter 10, Under the Floor   72

Chapter 11, Toilets   80

Chapter 12, Found   89

Chapter 13, Trapped   97

Chapter 14, Out   105

Chapter 15, Home   111

Chapter 16, The End   117

Non-fiction:

Going Underground, by Christopher Edge   121

For Val and Alex Grant

Chapter One
A Door

It is a door, I realise.

In the flickering, shadowing circle of my candlelight, there is a door.

I hear the voices again, the voices in the walls. I hold my candle to the edges of this long, narrow darkness, to the black wooden walls and the black wooden ceiling. I see faces in the grain of the wood: eyes, noses, mouths. I hear their voices and jab at them with my candle. They don't like the candle. The faces disappear back inside the wood.

I know this is a door because it is the shape and size of a door. But it's not like the doors in my house. It is brown, the darkest brown, and carved in four panels, studded with blackened nails. It is old.

There is a glinting gold handle and a black hole beneath it, a hole which is just the right shape for the thing in my hand. A key. (I know it is a key because I showed it to Eg and he told me what it was. But that was later.)

And then I hear them behind me. Footsteps, slowly at first. Walking.

One. Two. One. Two.

Then faster, louder. Marching.

One, two, one, two.

A light in the darkness behind me, growing bigger, brighter, nearer.

And faster. One two one two. Running.

And then there come the voices, roaring.

And the sound of my breathing.

In. Out. In.

I watch my shaking hand push the key into the keyhole. I turn the key and, with a grinding clunk, something has loosened. Dust falls through the circle of my faltering candlelight.

I turn the handle.

I push.

The door swings smoothly open and a gasp of air escapes. My candle flickers and dies.

Darkness.

This isn't the beginning of my story. But this is where I had to start it.

Eg said so.

Chapter Two
Up the Down Stairs

I've never written a story before. Actually I've never even read one before. Eg tells me this is unusual. He says a story is like real life but made up – true but not true. I haven't the faintest idea what he's talking about. This story (if it is a story) is not made up. It is true fact. So let me tell you the true facts.

It was a cold winter morning. I was shivering at my desk in the Learning Room, looking at my Learning Book. Hundreds of pages all in my mother's neat black handwriting. Everything is there that anyone could ever need to know, all bound up in hard, black leather.

Mother lit the fire as I sharpened my pencil, smoothed my exercise book open and straightened my ruler. She picked up the Learning Book and selected a page.

'Here we are, dearest angel,' she said, turning her mouth up at the corners. 'Addition, subtraction, multiplication and division. All the sums a boy could wish for.' She spread her bony fingers round my arm and squeezed. 'And why are we doing sums, my precious lamb?' she asked.

'I don't know, Mother,' I replied. Her grip tightened.

'And why don't you know, my precious lamb?'

'Because we do not ask why, Mother.' Her grip tightened further.

'And why do we not ask why, my precious lamb?'

'Because we do not need to know, Mother.' Her grip tightened even more and I felt my arm pulsing against her fingertips.

'And?'

'Because Mother knows best, Mother.'

'Good boy,' she breathed. Her hand fell away and I breathed too.

Mother was in a bad mood. I could tell by the number of sums she had given me. Hundreds of them. I remember glancing out at the rain and wondering what time I would be allowed in the garden. It would not be until much later. I hoped it was not me who had annoyed her. I quickly began my work.

Sometimes I did reading and writing in the morning then sums in the afternoon. And sometimes, like today, it was the other way round. I used to do other things when I was little. I remember there was once a map on the wall of the Learning Room. Lots of different places in lots of different colours, all surrounded by a blue sea. Then one morning it was gone.

I used to learn about the past. I remember something about a group of people who lived in a city a long time ago and one day they came to this land. They watched people fight till they died and they built roads. And I remember a fat king with a beard who had quite a lot of wives, but he didn't like any of them. So he killed them. And all of this had been in my Learning Book, but one day it wasn't any more.

'Never look back, only forward!' my mother said if I tried to turn back to where those pages had been torn out of the book. And then she would lean on the open book with my fingers caught between the pages until I had to pull them out and blow on them to stop the pain.

'Reading and writing and sums. Nothing else is needed, necessary or useful. The world is a dangerous place,' she would say. 'And what you don't know cannot hurt you.'

I finished my sums just before lunchtime and looked round at the closed door of the Learning Room. White and flat and smooth and closed tightly shut. And I waited.

I had no idea what Mother did while I was learning. I knew that in the evenings she and Father sometimes listened to the Box – a metal and wooden box in the sitting room that played music and voices to entertain you. But that was only in the evenings, after I'd gone to bed.

I knew she must be in the house somewhere because I could see the door to the garden from my desk. It was the only door to the outside and she had not gone through it. (A picture came in my head – Mother slipping into the garden. All big owl glasses and bony black dress and white spider hands scaling the high garden wall. It made me laugh.) And so I waited for her to come back to the Learning Room with my lunch.

I looked down at the Learning Book. My fingers played with the corner of the page of sums. My fingers stroked the edges of the closed, forbidden pages. My fingers edged between two pages and prised them slightly apart. I lowered my head to the desk and peered into the book. A page of spellings, a page of sums and the torn stubs of three pages that had been removed.

'Never look back!' shrieked my mother's hot breath on the back of my neck. One hand slammed the book shut and the other dropped a plate of sandwiches on the desk. I sat on my hands and shook. 'Only look forward,' she said, calming herself and stroking the cover of the Learning Book.

'Mummies,' she announced loudly, 'have one or two special tricks to make sure their little angels do not disappoint them. And telling Father that you have disappointed me,' she added, her voice dropping to an ominous whisper, 'is one method we hope we *never* have to use.'

I shuddered. Father is a man who travels in shadow, lives behind doors. I sometimes hear him clearing his throat or rustling papers but, just when I think I might catch a glimpse, he's gone. Mother says he does not like the noise I make.

Sometimes he calls me into his study and looks at me. Perhaps he's reminding himself of what I look like. Sometimes I think he may be about to say something. But then he sends me to bed with a flick of his finger.

'Spellings to be copied and learnt this afternoon,' said Mother, opening the Learning Book and selecting a page. 'Numbers one to three hundred. You will be tested tomorrow morning,' she said. 'I shall mark these *very* carefully,' Her black eyes closed in their dark hollows. 'And we shall see what you deserve.' Her voice grew colder. 'We always get what we deserve, don't we, my special angel?'

The smooth, white, flat door of the Learning Room swung shut behind her.

Darkness was creeping into the room when she next came to see me. I was allowed one hour in the garden. *Tick tock*, said the hall clock.

The garden air was cold and stung as I filled my lungs with it. I ran across the broad, neat grass in all directions, warming my stinging pink skin. I spun round and round, my arms flailing at the flower beds and bushes. I came to a stop looking to the bottom of the garden, to the dark place where I did not go. Where I must not go. Tall trees crowded together in shadow, their bare branches scratching against the darkening sky. Clawing and groaning, creaking and whispering.

I turned away, ran to my spade – last year's birthday present – and headed to a hole I had started two days earlier. It was over half a metre across and nearly a metre deep now. I looked up at the garden wall. Brick after brick reached to the sky. The wall stretched out from the house and curved into the dark place at the bottom of the garden, surrounding me. I looked up at the oval of sky above me and down at my hole. Clouds were gathering, spreading red and orange and purple blackness.

I climbed into the hole and began to dig.

When my arms were aching and the cold was biting at my sweat, I paused and puffed in cold air, puffed out hot air. Something was shining at me. Something was glinting in the red of the sunset beneath a green bush just a metre away. I looked away and back again. I glanced at the house. No sign of Mother or Father. I walked to the bush, bent down and saw it dangling among the leaves. A gold chain, like a necklace. Hanging on the end of it was a dark metal stick with teeth at one end and a ring at the other, which the gold chain was threaded through. I unhooked the treasure from the bush and slipped it into my pocket. My eyes twitched nervously to the house, to the windows.

I dug some more, pausing occasionally to pat my pocket and glance up to the house.

Mother called me. Time to go in. Wash, supper and bed.

I can always tell what kind of mood Mother is in at washtime. A good mood means I have a nice, hot bath with plenty of strong blue soap while she puts my clothes in the washing machine and sterilises my shoes, then a warm towel, a hot supper and pyjamas in front of the fire. A bad mood means ten minutes bent over the sink, face down in cold grey water.

That day was a very bad mood. The water was yesterday's, grey with a film of scum floating among the broken ice. The towel was cold and rough and damp across my bare shoulders. As she held my head down and scrubbed in each ear with the washing-up brush, I said, 'Mother, are you cross with me?'

She stopped scrubbing. I could hear her breathing.

'Cross, my special boy? Why would Mummy be cross?'

'I don't know, Mother.'

'No,' she said, 'you don't.' She pulled me up by the hair and scrubbed at my face with the towel. 'There. Nice and clean.'

She brought me a bowl of cold soup, which I ate alone in the Learning Room, a spoon in one hand, patting the treasure in my pocket with the other. In the dark silence, in the light of the flickering fire, I waited to be sent up to bed. But Mother did not come. I lit a candle and took it upstairs.

Once my bedroom door is shut, it does not open until the morning. That is the rule. I closed it behind me and sat on the floor of my attic room.

I took the treasure from my pocket and dangled it in front of my eyes. It twirled and glistened in the candlelight. Silently, I leaned forward and gently pulled at the floorboard in front of the door, loosening and prising it up.

Here, in the floor, on a ledge, was where I kept all my special things.

There was an envelope I'd been sent when I was tiny by some people called Aunt Heather and Uncle Doug. When it arrived it had a picture inside: a picture of a big cake and some writing. Mother took that for safekeeping. But I kept the envelope with its little picture in the corner and its sloping writing.

There was Bear, a toy I used to take to bed every night until Mother said I was too old. I begged and begged for one more night but she refused so the next night I told her I'd taken him in the garden and buried him. She believed me, I think. But my ears got double time with the washing-up brush for a week.

And now here was something very special to add to my collection.

I lowered the treasure in by its chain and watched as it came to rest, the chain coiling around it. And then I watched as the chain slipped away off the ledge and pulled the treasure after it. And I watched as they both disappeared into dark oblivion. And, for the first time I can remember, I wanted to cry.

I lowered the candle into the darkness. I could see the ledge on which I kept my treasures and the gap down which my new treasure had disappeared. I got on all fours and pushed my head through the space in the floorboards. Very carefully, I squeezed the candle in beside me, trying not to set my hair on fire. Down, down in the darkness I could see the faint glint of treasure.

I lay on the floorboards and pushed myself in further, deeper, up to my waist. I stretched for that glint of light. And then I realised I was sliding, and my waist, my knees then my feet were following me down the hole, into the darkness. On my back, head first, bumping up, bumping down, through the darkness. I think I was falling down the stairs on the other side of my bedroom door, down the up stairs – or was it up the down stairs? I was *inside* the stairs, falling *through* the stairs, into a heap at the bottom.

Amazingly I was still holding the candle. Even more amazingly, it was still alight. I got up on my knees and held it above my head. There, through a distant hole in the darkness, I thought I could see the shadows of my bedroom. But here, around me, was my candle's halo of light, and blackness. Nothing but blackness.

I found the treasure chain on the ground and slipped it in my pocket. I knew that was a good idea. And I knew that getting back up to my bedroom was a good idea. But they were the only two good ideas I had. How to get back up the down stairs, I had no idea.

I tried to pull myself back up what I thought were the stairs. I heaved and tumbled and fell back down with a thump. Then I heard something shift. I held my breath and felt the darkness deepening. I looked up to see the hole in the blackness above me close. The loose board in my bedroom floor had fallen back into place.

I thought about calling for help but decided it was probably better to die of hunger in the dark than to let Mother know what had happened. So I just stood there, turning in circles, holding out my candle and looking for a way out.

Then I noticed a crack between two pieces of darkness. I moved my candle closer. It was a narrow corridor, narrower than me, between two bare brick walls.

I scraped sideways between the rough bricks, turned a sharp corner and edged through the darkness. A thick spider's web pressed itself against my face. The corridor was so narrow that I couldn't lift my arms, couldn't get a hand up to wipe it away. The spider climbed over my nose and disappeared into my hair. I pushed on.

I came to another corner and scraped myself round it. And paused.

The space was so narrow both my ears were pressed against the walls – and I thought I could hear voices.

There were voices in the walls. Distant, loud, shouting voices. It sounded like arguing. I stumbled on, but then the arguing voices stopped and I thought I heard one of them say, 'What was that? Did you hear that?' And there was a distant tapping as though someone was knocking on a faraway door.

I moved as fast as I could, banging my knees and scraping myself between the bricks until the ground gave way to a steep slope. I tripped and stumbled out of the narrow brick corridor into a kind of tunnel, the walls and ceilings lined with black wood. I walked into the darkness, with the circle of light from my candle, on and on for what felt like miles.

And then there was a different darkness ahead of me. A solid rectangle of darkness.

It was a door, I realised.

A darkest brown door, carved in four panels, studded with blackened nails. There was a glinting gold handle and a black hole beneath it, a hole that was just the right shape for my treasure: a key.

And then I heard them behind me. Footsteps, slowly at first. Walking.

One. Two. One. Two.

Then faster, louder. Marching.

One, two, one, two.

A light in the darkness behind me, growing bigger, brighter, nearer.

And faster. One two one two. Running.

And then there came the voices, roaring.

My shaking hand pushed the key into the hole. I turned it and, with a grinding clunk, something loosened.

I turned the handle.

I pushed.

The door swung smoothly open and a gasp of air escaped. My candle flickered and died.

Darkness.

But even in the darkness the footsteps didn't stop. Faster and faster, closer and louder. The roaring voices were getting louder and I fumbled blindly for the key. I felt my way round the door and slammed it behind me. Somehow I got the key in the hole on this side, turned it, and the door was locked.

I stood in the darkness and listened to my heartbeat and my breathing and the voices from the other side fading into the distance.

Chapter Three
Eg

I don't remember much about what happened next. And that was the problem – or rather it turned out to be the problem.

I remember standing frozen in blind blackness. I remember fumbling for the candle, wishing I had a box of matches.

I remember putting the key in my pocket, and I remember walking. I walked through black empty echoes. I stumbled up pitch-dark stairs on my hands and knees then banged my head at the top. I pushed what I thought was the ceiling and found myself smothered under something like a blanket, swallowing a mouthful of dust and spiders. And then I was in a room. A grey room, swirling in specks of dust and half-light. I definitely was not in my own house any more. And I remember a door to a corridor, and another door.

I began to run but every door I ran through took me to another corridor, and another door. More stairs. Another door. The grey walls flew past me, and I banged through door after door after door.

And then at last fresh air. White light. Space. Sky. Clouds. Buildings. I stood and breathed and looked around me. Wherever I was, I had arrived.

Behind me was a vast grey building. Ahead tall metal railings stretched into the distance, interrupted by a huge pair of black gates. And beyond the gates a whole world of grass and trees and hills and mountains and, peeking behind them, a new white sun spreading its light. It was the biggest, most beautiful, most terrifying thing I had ever seen. I wanted to laugh and scream and shout and run back the way I'd come and hide.

When I lowered my eyes from the brightening sky, I saw a man walking towards me. He wore dirty blue overalls and rattled a hefty bunch of keys in his clawed hand. He had a face like the toffee Mother and Father had given me one Christmas. I used to chew it for just a few seconds every evening and put it back on my bedside table, gathering tufts of hair which I picked off the next evening. The man's chewed-toffee, hair-tufted head blocked out the sun. My insides sank into my shoes.

'You're early,' he grunted, sniffing at me.

I tried to speak. I wanted to ask him who he was, where I was, what he meant. But nothing came out.

'You deaf?' he gurgled, poking a crusty finger into my ear. 'You're early,' he shouted, jangling his keys. I quietly clutched the key in my pocket for safety.

'Am I?' I managed to croak.

'Gates don't open till eight. You shouldn't come in till eight.' He jerked his face into mine. I stared dumbly at him.

'I should put you back on the other side of them gates,' he muttered. But he didn't. He straightened up. 'I'm watching you, boy,' he growled. 'Don't you try to sneak

16

inside.' He flicked his eyes at the grey building behind me. 'You don't go in till the bell goes, understand?' I realised he wanted me to nod. So I did. 'I'm watching you, boy,' he repeated, prodding me with a gnarled fingernail. He turned and limped away into the building, throwing a final sneer over his shoulder at me.

I stood and grew colder, waiting to hear a bell and wondering why I would want to go inside when it rang.

Eventually two figures approached the gates, pushed them open and came closer. Two girls. They stopped a few metres away from me, put some bags down on the ground and started talking. I tried to listen. It seemed they too were waiting for the bell. Soon after the girls arrived, four shouting boys came through the gates then two, four, six, eight more. And then more. And still they kept coming.

I backed away from the growing sea of faces and bodies and voices. I had never heard or seen so many people in one place. They all looked like me but different. Legs, arms, heads – they had all of those. But there was something not quite right, something …

Suddenly a shadow fell over me.

'You're in our place,' it said. A body about twice my height and three times my width stood in front of me. Slowly it lowered a powdery pink face and pushed it into mine.

'Yeah, I'm talking to you, spittle,' she said.

'I – I'm not – my name's not –' I could barely speak.

'Spittle's not your name,' explained her friend. 'It's where you'll end up if you don't move. Hoss spittle,' she cackled.

'You're in our place, spittle,' said the first girl again. The spiders of her eyes reared and dipped as she blinked her black lashes.

I stepped to the left.

'Other way,' was all she said. I stepped to the right.

'More.' I stepped more to the right.

'Bit more.' I took a bit more of a step to the right.

She nodded, and I breathed again.

Where I had been standing, the girl with the spider eyes and three other girls now waited. They ignored me. They ignored everything, including each other.

Then there he was. Smiling like a cheerful python, his blue eyes burning with interest through a pair of glasses. He tipped his head to one side, catching the morning sun on one lens, blinding me. When I could see again, he'd taken a step closer. And still he stared, those blues eyes scanning my hair to my feet and back again. I could feel a sweat breaking out beneath my clothes as he approached and said quietly, 'You're new, aren't you?'

The sweat dried. I couldn't explain it – I still can't – but suddenly everything felt like it was going to be all right.

'I – yes, I think I am,' I said. 'How did you know?'

'I'm Eg,' he said by way of an answer. 'Come on.'

I followed.

He asked me my name. I told him. I don't think he's used it ever since. 'Where are you going, boy?' he says. Or 'What do you think, boy?'

The crowds parted as we walked through. Nobody said anything to Eg. No one even looked at him. They just got out of his way. It's always like that with Eg. I've never really understood why.

'You join us at a most interesting time,' he said, marching onward.

'Do I? Have I?'

'Yes,' he replied, 'a most interesting time. You wouldn't know it to look at us, but the school is in trouble.'

'School?' I repeated. I'd heard the word before. Mother did not like school, I remembered her telling me that. I was beginning to think that I might not like it either. Eg flicked a quick glance at me but did not stop talking or walking.

'Order is crumbling,' he went on. 'Chaos is barking at our door.'

'Barking?' I repeated.

'Barking,' he said firmly. 'If you repeat everything I say,' he added, 'this conversation will take far too long.'

'Sorry.'

'No need to be sorry.' And on we marched.

'Where are we going?' I asked.

He stopped and looked at me. Those blue eyes burned.

'Registration,' he said. 'Then first lesson. You've never been to school before, have you?'

'No. How did you –?'

'The face,' he replied, 'tells me everything.'

We marched through a doorway into the big grey building.

'Are we allowed in here?' I stopped in the doorway but Eg marched on. 'A man told me we shouldn't go inside until a bell rings,' I called timidly after him.

Eg stopped and turned.

'What did he look like?'

'Wrinkly,' I said. 'And grumpy.'

'Gritts,' Eg said. 'You call him Mr Gritts to his face. He's the school caretaker. And the bell will ring …' He paused and looked at something on his wrist. 'Now.'

A bell rang.

Eg hurried on and I hurried after him.

'How did you know?' I puffed in wonder. 'How did you know it would ring then?'

Eg just smiled.

'Which class are you in, boy?' he asked.

I looked at him. He looked at me.

'Did they not tell you?' He seemed astonished. 'Your parents, I mean?'

I looked at him. He looked at me. Just as my face reached melting point, he spoke.

'How old are you, boy?'

I stared past him, my mouth opening and closing. He extended a finger and pushed my chin up until my teeth met.

'You look a little small for my class,' he winced. 'But I think you'll do.'

Do what? I wondered. And on we marched.

We arrived at a room full of rows of tables and chairs. We sat down next to each other at one of the tables.

'Normally, I sit alone,' said Eg. 'Today, you may join me at my desk.'

'Thank you,' I said gratefully.

I sat uncomfortably still and waited to see what would happen next. And slowly I didn't feel so lost and confused.

'Now,' he went on, 'you must observe our classmates. The creatures with whom we will share our day.'

A group of four girls and then three boys came in and sat in opposite corners of the room.

'Mice,' said Eg. 'A quiet and harmless species. Easy prey for larger creatures. They're far more scared of you than you are of them.'

While the noise from outside the room grew louder, we all sat in complete silence. I watched the Mice. I looked then looked away, looked then looked away. And each time I looked away, I realised I couldn't remember a single thing about them.

Another group of girls came in, talking quietly. Each had long black spikes of hair, sprouting like tentacles from their heads.

'Spiders,' said Eg without moving his mouth. 'Leave them alone, and they'll leave you alone.'

Three boys lumbered in, one huge, one tiny and one somewhere in between.

'Spuds.' Eg smiled. 'They travel and feed in groups. Observe the shaved head. Round and knobbled. Like a potato.' I'm not sure but I think he might have winked at me.

The Spud family fell into their seats and spilled across two tables.

'Pandas,' said Eg as four girls giggled into the room. Where their eyes were, it seemed like they had two black holes. The Pandas travelled in a cloud of scent, something like the air freshener Mother used in the toilet at home. They wafted to their corner and perched on the tables, chewing invisible food.

Two skinny boys loped in after them. Pale eyes in long, skinny faces darting suspiciously around the room.

'Rats,' said Eg. 'These are just two of a much larger colony, all with sharp little teeth and nervous whiskers. Avoid them,' he added, lowering his eyes to the desk.

A woman came into the room, a small, grey, hunched figure shuffling between the desks.

It seemed that only Eg and me noticed her. Everyone else carried on doing what they were doing.

Finally the woman stopped at a table at the back of the room. Her table was different from all the others. All of the tables, except hers, were set out in rows and had nothing on them. Her table was on its own, piled high with papers and books and boxes. As she piled more papers on top, several fluttered to the ground.

'Miss Tremmel,' whispered Eg. 'Our form teacher – and the crumbling backbone of the school. Say nothing and do not let her see you.'

I sank down in my chair and tried to look invisible.

Miss Tremmel seemed not to notice me. She sat facing us and threw books from one side of her table to the other until she found the one she wanted. Then she began to read out a long list of names. After each one, someone in the room said, 'Here.' And when everyone had had a go except me, it was over. A bell rang and we all got up.

'She didn't call my name,' I said.

'Well, of course she didn't.' Eg laughed. 'You don't exist.'

I think he saw the panic shiver through me.

'I mean as far as she is concerned, you don't exist,' he went on his usual comforting way. 'You're not on her list. Normally, I'm the last to leave, when the rush has died down. But today I think it a good idea if we put you among the crowd.' We all funnelled to the door. While I was shoved and bumped into the corridor by Spuds and Spiders and Pandas, Eg seemed to float in a bubble of space.

'Where are we going?' I asked nervously. A strange feeling was nagging at me.

'First lesson,' said Eg, striding on down the corridor.

'First lesson?'

'Geography with Mr Squatsby. Usually very dull but with occasional outbreaks of interest.' Eg took a sharp left turn, spinning on one heel of, what I suddenly noticed, were odd shoes – they didn't match.

'Geography?' I said.

'You're doing it again,' said Eg. 'You're repeating.' That strange feeling became a gnawing feeling.

Chapter Four
More Doors, More Stairs

There was a time when I thought I could lie to Eg.

It lasted less than ten seconds.

'Where have I come from?' I repeated, stalling for time. Eg nodded and smiled. My brain raced for something to say. He said nothing, but his eyebrows were beginning to rise as though floating away into space. I knew he knew.

'I don't know,' I said quietly. 'I mean, I know where I was yesterday … but I don't know how I got here … and I don't know how to get back …'

Eg just nodded.

'Time to go.' He set off again. 'First lesson,' he called over his shoulder. I followed. 'You can tell me about it at break,' he said, smiling.

I wanted to say, 'Break?' But I didn't.

We went to another room full of people. The Spiders and Pandas and all the others were there again. I wasn't sure if they were the same groups, but they looked the same. Eg dragged me through them and sat down at one of the tables. He pointed at the chair next to his. I sat down and wondered anxiously what would happen next.

A man with a long ginger beard came in and began to shout. Every time he shouted, his beard bounced up and down above his blue, spotted tie.

Eventually all the other people sat down. They got things out of their bags and put them on their tables: thin yellow books and pens and pencils. The man handed some pieces of paper around the class. When he got to our table, he stopped and stared at me. I stared back. I could feel the tips of my ears growing warm. I lowered my eyes, but I could still feel him staring and my ears getting hotter.

'He's new,' said Eg loudly and clearly. The man rolled his eyes.

'Chaos,' muttered the man. 'Utter chaos.' And he moved on.

'Say anything loudly enough,' Eg explained quietly, 'and they'll believe you.'

The man threw a yellow book on the table in front of me. It was full of blank paper.

'You write your name on the front,' said Eg.

I wrote my name.

'Both your names, boy,' said Eg. 'And "Geography" just there.'

I wrote 'Geography' where he was pointing.

'And your last name,' said Eg. 'Your surname.'

I looked at him. He looked at me.

'Smith,' he said. 'Your surname is Smith.' And then he whispered to himself what sounded like 'Curiouser and curiouser …'

Eg took the piece of paper he had been given and began to write quickly and neatly in his yellow book. He whispered as he wrote.

'Open your book. Take this pen. Look like you're reading the sheet,' he whispered, sliding it towards me. 'If he says anything to you, tell him you're new and you don't understand.'

I stared at the piece of paper like I wanted my eyes to burn holes in it. The man sat down at the front of the room at his own table. He began to write things in lots of different yellow books, moving them from one pile to another.

'Swap books,' said Eg after a few minutes. He took my yellow book and gave me his. He stared at my name on the front of my book then opened it and began to write.

'You're writing in my book,' I whispered.

'Well done,' said Eg, smiling.

I leant over. There, coming out of the end of Eg's pen, was my handwriting.

'But, how –?' I began.

'Practice.' Eg grinned. 'Now, look busy while I finish this off.'

By the time a bell rang and everyone started to leave, Eg had finished my work. Some correct answers, he'd explained, but not as many as him. You couldn't expect a new boy to get everything right. It was all in a perfect replica of my writing. The same thing happened in the next lesson, which was called French, I think.

I said to Eg as we left the second lesson, 'Why are you doing all this for me?'

'If you don't do any work you'll be noticed,' he said. 'Perhaps not today or tomorrow. But they do expect you to do some work at some point. And we do not want you to be noticed at this difficult time.' He marched ahead. 'Pandemonium is hammering at the door of our little school.'

'What do you mean, *pandemonium*?' I asked, that familiar strange feeling swelling in my stomach.

'Anarchy', said Eg. 'Bedlam. Chaos. Disorder. And so on. Do you understand?'

I didn't.

'Now it's breaktime,' he said. 'Come with me.'

We went outside, and Eg led me to the place where we had met.

'This was where I found you, I think,' he said. 'Now, tell me everything. How did you come to be here, on this spot?'

I told him all that I could remember: the key and the stairs, the tunnel and the door. The darkness. I told him about my journey through the school: the doors and the corridors, right up to meeting him, Eg.

'I see,' he said. Looking back now, I wonder why he believed me. Perhaps he didn't.

When I had finished, he went strangely silent and blinked so slowly I could have run round the school twice while he did it. But I didn't. I watched and waited.

'We must retrace your footsteps,' he decided at last.

'Where were you standing when you saw Gritts?'

I showed him.

'We will go in here.' He indicated a large wooden door behind us.

We went in. A grey corridor stretched ahead.

'Remember this?' he asked.

I nodded hesitantly.

We walked along the corridor, past doors and noticeboards, and came to a T-junction. Another corridor stretched to the left and to the right. I looked first one way and then the other. He raised his eyebrows. I looked left and right again. Eg shrugged.

'Every corridor,' he said, 'looks almost exactly the same. You were running. You were frightened. You had no idea where you were. Why would you look where you were going?' I opened my mouth. 'You wouldn't,' he said before I could speak. 'So we must think.'

A bell rang.

'Time for third lesson,' Eg sighed. 'Maths. We will return at lunchtime and see if we can work anything out.'

There were more lessons. I can't remember how many. Two, maybe three. I tried to tell Eg that what we did next wasn't maths; it was sums. But he said I was wrong. I suppose that's what happens when you come from one world to another. They call things different names. And the sums were different. I could do the ones Mother gave me in my Learning Book.

Lunchtime came eventually. The thought of food made me suddenly realise that I hadn't eaten anything since a bowl of cold soup the night before. I was starving. But Eg said we must explore first and then eat.

We went back to the large wooden door and the long corridor and the T-junction. We turned left.

'Remember anything?' asked Eg. I shook my head. We turned round and walked the length of the corridor to some stairs.

'I remember stairs,' I said.

'These stairs?' he asked.

I shrugged. Eg placed the palm of his hand across his forehead and was silent for a moment.

'Sorry,' I said.

'No matter.' Eg drew a sharp breath and he went up the stairs. I trotted after him. There was another corridor at the top. More doors. More stairs.

I felt weak with hunger and something like despair. 'I think I'm trapped here,' I said. 'I can't get back.'

'Do you want to go back?' Eg asked. 'Or do you think you might like it better here?

'I don't know what –' But I didn't know what I wanted to say.

'Or perhaps there is somewhere else you would rather be? Somewhere less … worrying,' said Eg to himself, looking into the distance.

'I've never been anywhere,' I replied. 'Only home. And here. Where else is there?'

'What will your parents say – if and when you finally get home?' he asked.

'I think they'll be cross,' I said quietly.

'Very cross?'

I nodded.

'Lunchtime,' he announced. And off we went to the school canteen where we shared everything they had left: one lightly burnt sausage roll followed by a bowl of sickly yellow soup. Eg told me it was called custard.

'One more lesson, and then we go home.' Eg smiled at me.

'Home?' I said. My heart sank.

'My home,' said Eg. 'You're staying with me while you're here, of course.'

Chapter Five
The Outside World

The final bell of the day rang and school ended. We set off for Eg's house. As we walked out of the school gates, I glanced back. There was a large wooden sign attached to the railings. On it, painted in scratched and peeling gold letters, was:

Dr and Mrs Crouchnail's College
for Young Gentlemen and Ladies
Ne Unquam Respexeris

I looked ahead. A winding path stretched down a steep hill through a dark, close mesh of trees. We joined the crowd walking away from the school.

Soon we were deep in the trees, winding and bending through the forest. The track was stony and steep. The forest was dark and the sky was darkening.

'What were you saying earlier?' I asked. 'About someone knocking at the school door?'

'Pandemonium,' he said.

'What did you mean?'

'You noticed the sign outside the school? Dr and Mrs Crouchnail? They are our headteachers. They own the school. Two days ago they disappeared. A marvellous thing, you might think.'

I didn't really think anything. But I didn't say so.

'However,' Eg went on, 'their disappearance has caused a number of problems. I asked Miss Tremmel about it. She denied it all. A worrying sign. I'm afraid that in the darker corners of the school, the teachers are losing control. I fear a breakdown of order. And, with it, something far worse. I don't promise it,' he warned with a smile and a wagging finger, 'but I fear it.'

'What's going to happen?' I asked anxiously.

'There is a girl,' he said, his voice taking on a gravelly tone, 'who two years ago joined the school at the same time as me. Her name is – or was – Petal.' He coughed or laughed or choked. 'She was a quiet little girl, with quiet hair and a quiet face. Quiet shoes and no voice at all. Never spoke. Never drew attention to herself. A Mouse. Some people are loud – loud on the outside. And they're no trouble at all. It's the ones who are loud on the inside … They're the ones you need to watch.' He raised an eyebrow.

'Well,' Eg went on, 'the moment I saw her I knew she was trouble. And yesterday I heard that she has changed her name and now wants to be known as "JackGirl". Yes, I know it seems unusual, but there you have it. I noticed today that she has started to dress differently, more … aggressively. And she has begun to gather new people around her. In particular, a group of Rats.

You remember the two I pointed out this morning? Little sharp teeth and thin whiskers sprouting beneath their sharp noses? They and their friends are, probably, among the least gentle and caring of our fellow students. I fear the worst.'

'What's going to happen?' I asked, that feeling swelling in my stomach again.

'Probably nothing.' Eg smiled. But he didn't look at me.

We emerged from the forest and the path divided into four fingers. The other people who had walked ahead of us divided and wandered off down three of the fingers. The fourth and final finger was an empty path that stretched to the horizon.

'This way,' said Eg. And we headed alone down the empty path. I paused and looked back up the hill. The forest spread as far as I could see – left and right and up and up to the grey school buildings perched on top of the hill. Everything – the school, the day, the past, Mother, Father and my home – seemed so, so far away.

The path wound on across the bald, brown earth until, there, in the distance was a little building: one red house with four windows and a door.

'Here we are,' said Eg. 'My house.'

'Are you sure your mother and father won't mind?' I asked.

Eg just laughed.

'No,' he said, 'I'm absolutely sure they won't.'

'I mean, what will you say? What will you tell them?'

'Nothing.' He grinned.

Eg turned the door handle and we went in.

The first thing I noticed was the smell. It was like old socks and eggs and dust and something else I still cannot name. In the hall, there were three black plastic sacks with rubbish spilling over the top and across the floor. A couple of tin cans rolled free and Eg kicked them into a corner. We went into the kitchen where the cooker was hidden by a tower of saucepans, piled high and balanced on an egg cup. By the sink, in a corner where the soap should have been, a mound of wet brown teabags grew blue mould. And as we walked I could hear our shoes sticking and unsticking themselves from the floor with every step.

'Cup of tea?' he offered.

'I've never had tea,' I said. Mother did not allow it. 'Is it nice?'

'*Is it nice?* It's the finest!' he cried.

I stared wide-eyed around me while he put the kettle on.

We went into another room. There was a Box in one corner – a bit like the one Mother and Father listened to after I had gone to bed. And around it a crowd of tea cups had gathered. There were plates of dried food scattered across one settee. I later discovered you could pick up the plates by the cutlery that had stuck to them. Clothes and towels and blankets were heaped on an armchair. And everywhere, among all of this, there were books, hundreds of books – some open, some closed – and sheets of paper scattered like leaves in autumn.

On the stairs, sitting on a bed of fluff, there was something that looked like a pie.

'Chicken pie. Dinner,' said Eg, taking hold of my sleeve. 'And this is my study.'

As he opened the door, I looked down. On the carpet, at the entrance to Eg's study, there was a perfectly straight line. I realised it was a line of dirt. Outside of the door, the carpet was a greenish cake of dirt and fluff. Inside, it was smooth and clean and pure green. We went in.

The walls were lined with shelves of neatly ordered books. In the very middle of the room was a large wooden desk. On it were two neat piles of paper covered in Eg's handwriting, and a flat black box. At the front of the desk, either side of where you put your legs, were hundreds of drawers: some large, some tiny, and the rest every other size in between. Apart from the desk, the room was entirely empty and tidy.

'This is where I work,' he explained. 'I must have order where I work. I'll make the tea.'

I wandered around and marvelled at all I saw.

'You've got a lot of books, Eg,' I called out to the kitchen.

'Do you like reading?' he asked.

'I've never really … that is we didn't …'

'Help yourself.' Eg appeared in the doorway with a cup of tea in each hand. He passed one to me, smiling. 'And there's the radio, and the television –' he nodded towards the room on the other side of the stairs – 'and the computer, of course.' He pointed at the flat, black box on his desk. 'Help yourself to everything!'

'What do they all … do?' I asked.

He looked at me, those eyebrows of his beginning to float.

'I'll show you,' he said finally. 'I'll show you how it all works. Everything.'

'But what about your mother and father?' I asked nervously. 'Won't they mind?'

Eg smiled. 'They're not here,' he said.

'But when they come home …'

'Come home?' he repeated. 'My mother and father are abroad. Or somewhere. Working. Or something. I don't expect them home for a number of years.'

'They've left you here all alone? For a number of years?' I stared at him in amazement.

'Most parents are far too anxious about their children,' said Eg. 'And mine know that I'm perfectly capable of looking after myself for a year or two. Or rather they *would* know it if they stopped to think about it for a couple of seconds.'

I glanced through the doorway at the pie on the stairs.

'I know, I know,' he said as though reading my mind, 'the house could be a little tidier … but you should have seen it before my parents left. It was like a Petri dish. They may never return,' he went on. 'They said they were considering staying away when I last heard from them. Don't mention that to anyone of course.'

'Of course.' I nodded.

Eg slurped his tea loudly and sat down at his desk. 'Now, let's think about your situation. Get a chair from somewhere and we'll think what's best to do,' he said, staring at the little grimed window beyond his desk. 'You know, I've read stories about mysterious doors and wardrobes with strange, new worlds on the other side.'

I found a small, hard chair in the hall and, after dragging it into Eg's study, sat down beside him. I sipped my tea and felt comfortably warm. And that was when I realised.

'Eg?' I said. He looked up at me, his blue eyes burning.

'Yes?'

'I don't want to go home,' I admitted. 'Mother will be … disappointed with me for coming here. So I'd like to stay. With you. If that's OK.'

'Of course it's OK!' said Eg, smiling. 'You're very welcome, boy.'

And then he looked down and was quiet for a moment.

'I'm sure we've got nothing to worry about,' he said, opening one of the smaller drawers in his desk. It was full of yellow pencils. He selected one, opened another even smaller drawer and pulled out a pencil sharpener. He opened a third drawer and sharpened his pencil into it.

'I expect everything will be back to normal tomorrow,' he said, laughing to himself. 'I'm sure Dr and Mrs Crouchnail will be at the school gates in the morning, welcoming their students with a friendly growl and a couple of spur-of-the-moment beatings.'

'Do you really think so?' I asked.

'No,' he said, stirring his tea with his pencil then chewing it thoughtfully. 'No, I don't.'

Chapter Six
Daylight Robbery

I woke up the next morning in a strange room. A pair of faded and torn red curtains glowed faintly with the dark light of a winter morning. I was in a huge bed, snuggled under a blanket, my cold nose poking out the top. I sat up and slowly remembered who and where I was.

Except for me and the bed, the room was empty: four red walls and dust-brown floorboards. Spiders' webs looped around the ceiling.

Eg's head appeared at the door.

'Breakfast's ready,' he said cheerfully. 'Do you like porridge?'

I got dressed and went downstairs where we ate thick, sticky white soup with a red blob of jam and drank hot cups of tea in Eg's kitchen. The tower of saucepans was one higher and the mound of teabags had spread.

'We must tidy up in here one day,' said Eg. 'I'm beginning to forget what colour the floor really is. Perhaps next month. Come on, boy.'

We headed out of the front door, along the path across the open, brown ground towards a grey sky and the school.

'Where I live, an egg is a kind of food,' I said. 'You boil it.'

'It's the same here,' said Eg, grinning kindly. 'You can also fry, scramble, or poach it.'

'But your name –' I began.

'Only has one "g",' he interrupted. 'It's an abbreviation. It's short for – a longer name.' He paused. 'You can imagine what they called me when I first came to this school.'

But I couldn't.

The school had not changed. Spiders and Pandas and all the others stood around outside in groups. Gritts the caretaker pulled an empty trolley across the concrete school yard. A small pack of Rats roamed around the railings snarling 'Get out the way' at anyone who came within a metre of them.

A group of three Spuds stood a little distance away from where we came to a standstill. I looked at the ground. But they all shouted 'Eg!' and suddenly he was surrounded by them, punching and pinching and wrestling him. He was laughing. I tried to smile.

'All right, boys?' said Eg.

'All right, Eg?' said one of the Spuds. When he spoke, his rubbery lower lip flapped up and down. And when he stopped talking it almost swallowed his flat nose.

'All right, Eric?' said Eg. 'Anything?'

'Nothing,' said Eric, shaking his dented, battered head. Eg pursed his lips and thought for a moment. We wandered on.

'You – you spoke to them,' I said after a while.

'Yes, I did.' Eg smiled.

'But I thought – I mean, yesterday you didn't speak to … any of them.'

'I was busy speaking to you,' said Eg, pausing and looking around. 'Eric and his friends may resemble bulldogs, but they're not quite as ugly as they look.' He spotted something and marched off. I followed.

Eg had arrived at another group, mainly girls, and began to talk to one. She was tall and thin with long, dark hair and seemed to be called Lulu.

'I've heard three different ones,' she was saying as I got close enough to hear. 'Firstly, they've been murdered.'

'Who would want to kill a pair of headteachers?' Eg wondered aloud.

'A lot of people might want to,' said Lulu.

'But who would actually do it?'

'You've heard what they're saying about Petal.' Lulu looked around at the school yard. 'And people are swearing there are bloodstains in at least three different places around the school.'

Eg nodded, frowning seriously. 'And secondly?' he asked.

'They've run off with all the money,' said Lulu. 'They've emptied the school piggy bank and gone to live on a desert island. Mrs Crouchnail was seen with a suitcase a couple of days ago, so the story goes.'

'And Dr Crouchnail in a flowery shirt?' Eg nodded thoughtfully. 'It's possible. Financial difficulties may have set in. Or they may have decided that lying on a hammock, sipping a cocktail is preferable to shouting at children all day and beating them. Each to his own,' Eg said, smiling. 'And thirdly?'

'Kidnapped,' said Lulu. 'A group of Spider girls reckon a ransom note came through the staff-room window yesterday, wrapped round a brick.'

'How much did it ask for?' Eg asked.

'Million, apparently,' said Lulu.

'And was it signed?'

'No news on that yet,' said Lulu, 'but I'm sure someone will have made something up by lunchtime.'

Eg laughed.

At this point I stopped listening because something sharp was sticking in the back of my neck. I turned round. A finger was pointing at me. A whiskered nose, sharp teeth and little black eyes were looking down at me.

'Got any money?' it squeaked. I think I saw something metal glinting in his hand.

'No,' I whispered hoarsely.

'Says he hasn't got any,' said the Rat. Two more rat faces appeared, one over each shoulder.

'Shall we hurt him?' said one. The first Rat smiled and showed me the knife he was holding.

'Like it?' he said.

'Lovely,' I croaked.

Eg appeared next to me. I thought he was going to say something. I thought he was going to rescue me. But he walked away.

'Empty your pockets,' said the first Rat, his nose sniffing and twitching at me.

I put my hands in my pockets, my fingers nervously closing around the key. If they took it, I would never be able to go home.

'Empty your pockets,' said the Rat again, leaning in.

In the other pocket, I found something I didn't know I had. I pulled it out and looked at it. It was a small circle of bright, gold metal with little pictures and words on it. The Rat snatched it and held it under my nose.

'Nice,' he leered, showing his sharp little teeth. He showed it to the other two Rats.

'Nice,' echoed one of the other Rats. The third one just whistled. And they turned on their heels, pushed Eg out of the way (he had unfortunately positioned himself directly behind them) and disappeared into the crowd.

Once I had stopped shaking and my breathing had settled, I told Eg what had happened, about the piece of metal.

'Did it look like this?' Eg asked, producing a bright circle out of his own pocket.

'Yes, it did!' I cried. 'I didn't even know I had it!'

Eg smiled.

'You didn't,' he said. 'Not until I put it in your pocket while you were talking to your new friends.'

'Clever!' I said.

'Oh, it's easy to put things into people's pocket,' said Eg. 'Taking them out of people's pockets – that's the difficult bit.' Looking over my shoulder, he began to laugh. The Rat with the knife was emptying his pockets, as if he had lost something. One of the others was looking for it on the ground. The third one was shouting at them both.

Eg flicked the bright circle of metal into the air, caught it and put it back in his pocket.

'He's new,' Eg called over to Lulu, nodding at me.

'New? Good timing.' She smiled.

We left as the bell rang and headed for registration.

'Murdered, kidnapped or thieves on the run,' muttered Eg to himself as we walked. 'Chaos barking at the door.'

'Why did that Rat boy pick on me?' I asked.

'Because you are new and vulnerable,' explained Eg. 'A sign of the dark times that are upon us. And if we do nothing then times will only become darker.'

'Eh?'

'A brilliant question,' said Eg. 'And one I am glad you've asked me. Dr and Mrs Crouchnail are well-meaning people. The school, we are told, is run for the good of its students. The teachers are kind and they like us. However, there are … rules.'

'What do you mean, *rules*?' I asked.

'If you do not work hard, you are beaten. If you do not do what you are told, you are beaten. If you are rude to a teacher or even under some circumstances another student, you are beaten. If you do something worse then something worse will happen to you. There is no tolerance. There is no leniency. There is no mercy.' Eg folded his arms and closed his eyes. 'With Dr and Mrs Crouchnail out of the way, all of these things will go unpunished. With Dr and Mrs

Crouchnail out of the way, everything and anything will go unpunished. Everything,' he repeated, raising a finger, 'and anything.

'So we have two problems,' he went on. 'Dr and Mrs Crouchnail have disappeared. You have arrived. Is there a connection? No, I don't think so.' He appeared to be talking to me. But he wasn't. He was talking to himself. 'How did you get here? Can we get you back? Notice I do not ask whether you want to go back. But there is no doubt that this is a terrible time to be here. A terrible time.'

I nodded.

'Anyway,' he said as we arrived at the form room, 'those are the problems.'

'So what do we do?' I asked.

Eg grinned.

'We solve them, boy,' he said, nodding vigorously. 'We solve them.'

Chapter Seven
The Worst

At breaktime later that day Eg and me were out in the
school grounds, sharing a bacon roll, when Lulu came
running at us.

'Have you heard?' she puffed.

One of Eg's eyebrows lifted a millimetre or so.

'Last lesson, there wasn't a class in the art room. It
should have been empty. But Miss Tremmel found Petal and
a couple of others in there when they were supposed to be
in French,' said Lulu, still panting. She rested a hand on my
shoulder while she got her breath back.

'And?' said Eg.

'And Miss Tremmel told them off.'

'It's not the biggest news I've ever heard, Lulu,' said Eg.

'That's not the news,' said Lulu. 'Petal says to her: "Me
and my friends aren't going to French. We're not going to
any more lessons. What are you going to do? Send us to the
headteachers? You can't, can you? Cos they're gone." And
Miss Tremmel tells Petal she's truanting and will have to face
the consequences and she goes off to get another teacher.'

'And what happened when Miss Tremmel came back?'
asked Eg.

'She didn't,' said Lulu.

'Didn't what?' asked Eg.

'Didn't come back,' said Lulu. 'According to my source, Miss Tremmel was found at the bottom of the stairs by the art room. Unconscious. Bleeding. Some people are saying one of Petal's Rats pushed her. That boy … what's-his-name … with the teeth.'

'Bunny?' said Eg.

'That's the one,' said Lulu. 'Others are saying he hit her. With a cricket bat.'

'Where is Miss Tremmel now?' Eg looked worried.

Lulu shrugged.

'Some say she's dead. Others say she's in the staff room all bandaged up and having a cup of tea.'

'And where is Bunny?'

'Around,' said Lulu. 'Just wandering around, looking nasty. Holding a cricket bat.'

'And Petal?'

'Still in the art room.'

'Oh dear,' said Eg gravely. 'Oh dear.'

Lessons were quiet for the rest of the morning. Mr Stent, the maths teacher, said nothing to us. We found sheets on our desks, one each, and instructions written on the board: 'Answer the questions on the sheet in silence.' Mr Stent did not speak for the entire lesson. He just sat strangely silent and looked at his books, occasionally glancing up at us. We sat strangely silent and looked at our books, occasionally glancing up at him. It was as though we were all waiting for something to happen. But nothing did.

It was the same in history with Mrs Buttle. Paper on the desks. Instructions on the board. Silence. Even Eg looked uncomfortable.

At lunchtime we went outside. Eg said he needed fresh air, not food. I watched him, breathing it in and thinking. I knew he was thinking because he wasn't talking and his mouth was twitching. He always does that when he's thinking. It's like he's chewing his brain over.

Finally he said to me, 'Look around, boy. What do you see?'

I looked around the school grounds. Nearby a group of Panda girls were standing and talking and putting stuff on their faces. A herd of Spuds were lumbering round and round the concrete, pushing sandwiches into their mouths and thumping each other and laughing. A couple of Rats were circling a group of Mice and laughing. Beyond that, hundreds of people were standing about and talking. It looked just the same as the day before.

'A load of people?' I eventually replied. 'And there's quite a lot of rubbish on the floor,' I added, wondering if that was important.

'Any teachers?' said Eg.

I looked around again.

I shook my head.

'Exactly,' he said. He strode away, towards the school building.

'Exactly what?' I asked, jogging after him.

'Where are they all? That is what I ask myself,' said Eg. 'There is always a teacher wandering around out here. Lately there have been two of them. Safety in numbers, I think. But why not now? Come on.' And he disappeared through the large wooden door into the school. I followed.

'Where are we going?' I asked.

Eg stopped and turned, pressing a finger to his lips. He smiled and jerked his head behind him at an empty corridor. He set off again and I followed him down the empty corridor, and then another corridor and then another. We climbed some stairs and eventually paused outside a narrow red door. Eg tipped his head towards it. We had arrived.

Eg took a piece of wire from his pocket, poked it in the keyhole and wiggled it around for a few seconds. Then he opened the door, pushed me in and closed the door behind us. We were in complete blackness. I could hear Eg rustling and shuffling until a little light appeared shining on his face. Along with everything else he ever needed, Eg had a torch in his pocket.

We were standing in a very small room, surrounded by buckets and brooms and mops. There were shelves full of bottles and tins and piles of cloth.

'Where are we?' I whispered.

'Gritts' cleaning cupboard,' hissed Eg. 'If he finds us, we're dead.'

I swallowed.

Shuffling slowly forward, Eg headed to the back of the cupboard. I followed silently in the dark, until I heard something move. I froze. The torch swung round just in time for me to see a mop topple to the ground. And land on a tin bucket. Which rang like a bell. Then tipped over. And rolled into a broom. Which tipped forward and banged into the shelves. Which rattled all the bottles. And swept them off the shelf, through the air and on to the floor where they rolled back and forward to an eventual standstill.

Silence.

'If he finds us,' repeated Eg very slowly and quietly, 'we're dead. So please, try to be careful.'

Stepping over the debris, Eg pressed his face to the wall at the back of the cupboard.

He turned and beckoned to me.

'Through there,' he whispered. 'Look.' He was pointing

to a little hole in the wall, about two centimetres across. I pressed my eye to it.

I could see a room with people in it. They were sitting in chairs, around a fireplace, mugs of tea cupped in their hands like precious gifts.

'Teachers!' I exclaimed quietly.

'Staff room,' said Eg. 'Notice anyone missing?'

I pushed my eye to the hole.

'Not sure,' I murmured.

'Miss Tremmel in there?'

I looked again.

'No,' I whispered.

'I thought not. Now, listen.' Eg pressed his ear to the wall.

I pressed my eye back to the hole and strained my ears.

A man was talking.

'That's Mr Squatsby,' whispered Eg.

'But are they coming back?' Mr Squatsby was saying. He looked around at the solemn faces, his long ginger beard curved limply over his stomach.

'Well, of course they are,' snapped a woman with blonde hair piled up like ice cream.

'Mrs Mant,' said Eg, pressing his ear even harder to the wall. 'French teacher.'

'Oh, are they?' Mr Squatsby went on angrily. 'How do you know? Where are they?'

Mrs Mant clutched her knees with her hands. 'I'm sure there's a perfectly sensible explanation.'

'Have you heard some of these perfectly sensible explanations?' said a man. I recognised him: Mr Stent, my maths teacher with the shiny bald head. 'Form 4B told me they'd been arrested. By the police. For shoplifting!'

'Armed robbery, according to 5D,' sighed Mrs Buttle, her face like a candle that had been left too close to the fire.

"Perhaps the question we should be asking is *can* they come back?' said an elderly woman with thick glasses.

'Miss Dribb, art teacher,' whispered Eg.

'Never mind where Dr and Mrs Crouchnail are,' she went on. 'They're not here, and we are. And we have lost Miss Tremmel because of it. We have a girl who has taken possession of my art room and will not give it up. Gangs are running wild and no one who is prepared to tackle the issue.'

'Close the school,' growled Gritts. He had been standing unnoticed in a corner, silently blending in with the peeling, brown wallpaper.

'And what would we tell the parents?' asked Mr Squatsby, smiling with thin lips. 'Sorry, dear parents, but we've misplaced two headteachers and lost control of the school? Do you not think they might want their school fees refunded, Mr Gritts?'

'Just saying,' mumbled Gritts bitterly. 'Going to my cupboard. You might have lost control but that's no reason for mess.'

And he disappeared from sight. I heard him close the door on his way out.

I turned to Eg. But he was gone. And so was the torchlight.

'Hello?' I whispered into the darkness.

Silence.

'Eg?' Panic was rising within me.

The door opened. Light poured in.

It was Eg, letting himself out.

'Quickly,' he said. 'Gritts will be here soon and we don't want to get in his way.'

'Shouldn't we tidy up before we go?' I asked.

'I have,' said Eg, locking the door as swiftly as he had unlocked it.

We hurried silently away down the corridor.

We knew that something was wrong before we got outside. There was music. Trumpets and drums thumping and blaring and echoing from the school buildings. We could hear it in the corridors.

Outside it was twice as loud. Hundreds of people had gathered. It looked like the whole school was there. A crowd of heads as far as the school walls shouted and cheered while music filled the cold, grey sky. In the distance, a path was clearing. People were stepping to one side. You could see the grey concrete appear as they parted. And in the distance, marching towards us, a cluster of bodies.

'It's her,' said Eg. 'It's Petal.'

He pointed to a girl being carried on a heavy, black wooden chair through the crowd. It looked like two broomsticks had been threaded under the legs of the chair. At either end of them were four boys, carrying the chair at shoulder height. Around her walked more boys – Rat boys. One of them was carrying a cricket bat over his shoulder. Some of the others had pieces of wood that looked like broken table legs. One had a large black box perched on his shoulder from which the music was pounding.

As the procession drew closer, the crowd became louder and the figure of the girl on the chair grew clearer. Her raven-black hair was piled high on her head, scooped and swirled into a bulge like a bullet. Even as the chair wobbled and dipped, her face was calm, almost blank. She stared straight ahead as though she did this kind of thing most days and was bored with it.

Closer and closer she came until she was looming over us in her chair. The procession paused to open the large wooden door behind us. She looked down at Eg. He looked back at her, his face like stone.

'What are you doing up there, Petal?' he asked.

'The name,' she spat back at him, 'is JackGirl.'

And she was gone, carried through the door.

Eg remained unusually silent for the rest of the afternoon.

I asked him what was wrong.

'The worst has come to the worst,' was all he said.

After school we went back to Eg's house.

'Eg,' I said as we drank a cup of tea on the settee, 'why is Petal doing this?'

'Power,' he replied without a moment's thought. 'When Dr and Mrs Crouchnail disappeared, there were two likely outcomes. Either the other teachers would step in and run the school – or this. The teachers seem to be in a state of helpless shock. So there is power up for grabs. And she has started to grab it. Her gang of followers will grow, all of them hoping for a bit of that power. Everybody likes a little power over someone else.' He paused and smiled sadly to himself.

'Why it should be *her*, I don't know' he went on. 'Her mother is a piano teacher, you know. I went for two or three lessons at her house when I was younger. But we had a disagreement, Petal's mother and I. She's a *very* difficult woman.'

He finished his tea, showed me how to work the television then disappeared into his study.

I sat alone and watched the pictures on the television for the rest of the evening. At first it was fascinating. I watched a programme about a family that shouted at each other a lot. Like everything else since I got here, it seemed strange and different and I thought how exciting my life had become since I met Eg.

I watched a few more programmes about people who shouted a lot. Then I watched something called the News, which was about a terrifying place I had never heard of. And I began to feel strange and uncomfortable, and things didn't feel so exciting any more, just frightening. I thought that maybe I didn't want to stay here and maybe I wanted to go home after all.

And then I remembered something.

'Never look back,' I said to myself. 'Only forward.'

Chapter Eight
The Throne

Eg and me walked to school the next day beneath growling black clouds. As we reached the hill and walked up through the forest, it was clear that things were changing. Yesterday's silent procession of grey faces had become a thundering sprawl of glowing faces and teeth. Spiders scuttled and surged and screamed. Spuds barged and shoved, wrestled and played leapfrog, scattering little Mice off the path and into the trees. A group of Pandas sang a song as they walked, brushing their hair in time to the tune. Three girls who I did not recognise glided serenely past us. Each looked exactly the same, their charcoal-black hair scooped and swirled and piled high on their heads like –

'Bullets,' said Eg, smiling grimly.

'They look just like … just like … *her*,' I whispered.

'You can say her name,' said Eg. 'Her name is *Petal*,' he added loudly.

'But why do they want to look like Petal?' I asked.

'It's called fashion,' said Eg. 'If you can make yourself *look* like someone then maybe there's a chance that you can *become* like that someone.'

'But why do they want to be like her?'

'Fear,' Eg replied firmly.

'Oh, I see,' I said. But I didn't.

'The time will soon come, boy, when everyone in the school will be either for her or against her. Most will be for her. And when she triumphs, when she takes control of the school, they will be safe.'

'What will happen to those who were against her?'

'Well, let's just hope it doesn't happen,' said Eg. So I did.

We walked through the school gates into a swarm of Rats who spat and glared at us. I kept my head down and tried to walk wide of them.

'Good morning, gentlemen,' I heard Eg say. 'How lovely to see you all again.'

He strode past their open mouths and patted one on the cheek.

We hurried on, past another group of bullet-headed girls, giggling and chattering and stroking each other's hair. Past a Spud kneeling on another Spud, punching him in the face. Past a Rat with a boy's head under his arm, dragging him screaming round and round in a circle. Past a Panda girl, sitting alone on the ground and crying.

'I think we'll go in a little early for registration today, shall we?' said Eg.

Our classroom was empty when we arrived. We sat in our usual seats and waited. Eg was silent.

I turned to Eg. 'Do you think Miss Tremmel will turn up?'

He shook his head but remained silent.

'What are you thinking about?' I asked after a while.

'I am thinking about what I'm going to think about,' he said, putting his fist under his chin and sighing with a look in his eyes like he wasn't there any more.

'You're deciding what you're going to think about?' I asked, mystified.

He sighed again but said nothing.

There was a rumbling from the corridor. A crowd of people charged past our door and the rumbling faded into a shrieking distance.

The bell rang but Miss Tremmel did not come to do the register. No one did. After a few minutes, Spiders, Pandas, Spuds and everyone else barged in around and past us. They stood and roamed and fought and shouted, while Eg sat perfectly still and silent, and a wall of noise rose up around us.

The bell for the end of registration sounded. The noise climbed a note or two. And everyone left, pushing and tripping out the door, leaving the two of us alone.

'What now?' I asked.

'Art,' said Eg. 'Art with Miss Dribb. Come on, boy.' He stood up. 'Let's go and see what's what.'

We reached the stairs to the art room. I paused for a minute at the bottom, thinking of Miss Tremmel tumbling down those stairs and Bunny the Rat at the top, laughing and shouting down at her crumpled body. We climbed the stairs.

There was a notice on the art room door. It said: *Art lessons will be in Room 7 today.*

Eg stared at it.

'Where's Room Seven?' I said.

Eg continued to stare.

And I realised it was not the notice that held his attention. It was the glass in the door. He was staring through it. I shuffled alongside him to have a look.

There in the art room, in a corner on the teacher's desk, was a chair. But it was not like a chair. Cardboard or wood cut into scrolls and painted gold had been attached to the arms and to the back. Glued to the chair in fancy patterns were glass beads, red and blue and green and purple. Some kind of fur or cotton wool had been used to trim the edges. It was like … like a *throne*.

And on it sat Petal. She was facing away from us, staring out of a tall window, looking down to the ground below. On either side of her stood two Rat boys, arms folded, top lip curled. Another group of Rats sat round a table playing cards. Four girls, all with black bullet hair piled high on their heads, were chewing invisible food and talking. Each one held a notebook and pencil as though waiting to write something down.

Petal looked away from her window and called one of the Bullet girls over. The Bullet girl nodded and came to the door. I stepped away and pretended to be looking at something very interesting on the floor. Eg stared straight into the girl's eyes. She stared back.

'JackGirl says you gotta come in,' she told him, tucking up the corners of her pinched lips into a smile.

'Delighted,' said Eg, pushing past her into the room. Petal ignored us. She just sat there staring out of her window. I wandered behind while Eg strode straight to the window.

'So –' began Eg.

'You have been staring through my door,' said Petal.

'Yes, Petal, because –' Eg started to say.

'Your art lesson has been moved,' she went on. 'Miss Dribb has had to be relocated. I require this room for my use, for my … purposes.'

'What exactly are your purposes, Petal?' asked Eg, taking a step forward. A Rat took a step forward to meet him.

'You know,' said Petal very firmly. 'And you know perfectly well that is no longer my name. You know what my name is. Please use it. Unless, of course, you would prefer to call me … Highness?'

Eg laughed. Petal did not.

'Come here,' said Petal. 'Come and look here.' She indicated the tall window through which she had been looking.

'See?' she said. Eg looked down. I looked over his shoulder. The window looked across the school grounds to where a ramshackle gang of Rats were roaming, their eyebrows hunched low over black holes. A group of girls were wandering around, aimlessly chatting. A pair of Spuds were sitting together on a low brick wall, sharing a bag of crisps.

As if on a signal, each and every one of the Rats looked up at our window. Petal raised a hand to them, pointed to the Spuds and closed her fingers into a fist, as if crushing them in the palm of her hand. Immediately the Rats homed in on the Spuds and enclosed them in a wall of pistoning elbows and kicking legs. The scrum moved across the school yard, through a door and into the school building as the sound of a muffled scream echoed and died away. All that remained was an empty bag of Ready Salted blowing away across the ground and a trail of broken crisps.

'You see?' Petal smiled. 'The children are becoming lazy without proper supervision. Some people feel that they do not have to go to lessons.' Her smile fell. 'They are wrong.'

'And what will you do when Dr and Mrs Crouchnail return?' asked Eg. 'How will you explain –'

'Who would care if you were to disappear, Eg?' she asked, cutting him off. 'And you, you funny little boy,' she said, pointing at me, 'who would care if you were never seen again? No one. No one in the world. So do be *careful*,' she warned, curving her mouth into something like a smile. 'Be *good*.'

She laughed quietly to herself.

'Now, I believe you have an art lesson to go to,' she announced. 'You may leave.' And with that she turned back to her window. 'Bunny, pop to the dinner ladies, would you, and see if my grapes have arrived.' She was talking to one of her guards, one of the Rats. She did not look at him. He did not move or look at her. But his eyes opened a little wider and he nodded.

'Tell them I do not like tinned peaches,' Petal went on. 'A tinned peach is not a grape. And I want grapes. Do you understand, Bunny? If you return with tinned peaches again, you will join our friend in the cupboard for an hour or two.'

We left.

'What's going on?' I asked as we walked along the corridor to Room 7.

'*JackGirl* –' Eg almost retched the name – 'is building her kingdom. Already we are at the stage where it will be difficult to remove her from her throne. And the longer it goes on, the harder it will become. Until she can never be removed.'

'But why … why …?' I struggled to find the question let alone the answer.

'Why is she running the school like a teacher?' said Eg. 'Why doesn't she cancel all the lessons and have a big party where everyone runs wild and does what they want? Because she is clever,' he explained. 'If the school falls apart then there will be no school. And without the school, she has no power. No, she will keep things just the way they have always been. Except that she will be in control.'

We arrived at Room 7, knocked and entered. Eg said we were very sorry to be late but that we had been held up. Miss Dribb did not seem even slightly concerned – just relieved that we had turned up at all. She pointed to a tea cup and saucer on her desk and told us to draw them. Meanwhile, she sat behind her desk and looked pale grey and anxious.

I began to draw. I liked drawing. It was one of the only lessons where I didn't have to get Eg to do my work for me.

I was just shading the cup handle when I noticed Eg. He had drawn nothing and had chewed the top of his pencil away. His lips were covered in tiny wooden splinters. For the first time ever, I saw that he was worried. I felt a cold weight hit the bottom of my stomach.

'What are we going to do?' I asked.

He turned and looked at me.

'It's not normally like this,' he said, trying to smile. 'We'll soon put things right and then you'll be happy to stay here. Normally it's quite safe and boring and happy.' Again he tried to smile but the corners of his mouth seemed too heavy.

'You keep saying that,' I mumbled. 'You keep saying we'll put things right, we'll solve the problems, we'll work it all out and everything will be safe and fine. But we never *do* anything. You never actually *do* anything, you just … sit there and *think*.'

Miss Dribb was looking at me, eyebrows raised. I realised I had been shouting.

'And what do *you* suggest we do?' whispered Eg angrily.

'Find Dr and Mrs Crouchnail, of course,' I said.

'How?' he asked.

I said nothing.

'It's not a very detailed plan, is it?' said Eg. 'We can all crash and stumble around and moan and shout. But without a plan we will solve nothing.'

'And do *you* have a plan?' I whispered.

'Several,' he replied.

Chapter Nine
The Assembly

Finally at breaktime Eg stopped his endless thinking and spoke.

'So,' he said as we headed outside, 'this is what we're going to do.'

But there was no chance for him to tell me. Lulu, the thin girl with the long black hair, came charging up to us.

'News,' she said, panting. 'Three new theories. One, Dr Crouchnail has killed Mrs Crouchnail and is now on the run from the law. Two – and I heard this one completely separately – Mrs Crouchnail has killed Dr Crouchnail and *she's* on the run from the law.'

Eg smiled. I think it was the first time he'd done it all day.

'There's a similarity in those two stories,' he said. 'Which I think means we can ignore them both.'

'That's not all,' said Lulu. 'Three, alien abduction. According to Nostril, Gritts the caretaker saw a large saucer-shaped flying craft land in school a few nights back. He saw Dr and Mrs Crouchnail climb aboard.'

'Who's Nostril?' I asked.

'A boy in the year above us,' said Eg. 'Very large nostrils. Slightly smaller brain. Anything else, Lulu?' he added.

'Yeah, two things,' she said. 'One, the story about them running off with all the money is doing the rounds again. Apparently, there's a safe or a vault or something hidden in the school where they kept all the money. You know, cash, gold, jewels, riches beyond your wildest dreams.'

'I've heard that story before,' said Eg, getting that faraway look in his eyes.

'People are saying Gritts went to check on it and found the cupboard was bare,' said Lulu. 'Not a penny left.'

'Interesting,' said Eg. 'And the second thing?'

'Yeah.' Lulu nodded. 'I saved the biggest for last. The rumour is that JackGirl's holding an assembly after lunch.'

'W-what?' stuttered Eg in a hoarse whisper. 'How do you mean, an assembly?'

'An assembly,' explained Lulu as if it didn't need explaining. 'You know, we all go into the hall, sit down, someone talks at us, we pretend to listen, they stop, we get up, we leave. An assembly,' she repeated, just to make it clearer.

'An assembly?' said Eg.

'You're getting the hang of this,' said Lulu. 'Yes, an assembly.'

'JackGirl? Petal?'

'Yes, Eg.'

Eg fell silent and stared at the ground.

'And you don't think it's *strange*?' he said.

'I don't think it's *true*,' said Lulu.

But it was true.

At the end of lunchtime, people began to gather in the school yard by a large pair of doors. Then the crowd separated and formed a series of parallel lines, as everyone got into their form groups. Teachers marched up and down at the head of the lines. Rats patrolled among them, sneering and shoving the lines into straight silence.

Eg and me sat on a stone step and watched from a distance.

'That's the hall,' said Eg, nodding towards the building in front of which the lines were forming.

'Are *we* going to the assembly?' I asked.

Eg paused and thought.

'Yes, of course we are.' He stood up suddenly, breathed in deeply through his nose and walked to the back of the line of our form group. I followed.

As we joined our form, the teachers and Rats had started letting the groups into the hall. By the time we went in, the hall was half full. Chairs were set out in rows, in two blocks with an aisle between them. At the front there was a raised wooden platform with a pair of dusty, blue velvet curtains on either side. It was empty. So we sat in expectant silence and looked at the space on the stage where something might happen.

The hall doors were closed as soon as we were all sitting down. The teachers sat in a row at the edge of the hall, looking across us. The Rats sat in a row of chairs in front of the stage, staring back at us. Eg looked from the Rats to the teachers, then from the teachers to the Rats, and raised an eyebrow and shook his head.

'You!' shouted one of the Rats, standing up. He was pointing at Eg. 'Yeah, you! Seen something you're not happy with?'

'Me?' said Eg, standing up to reply. 'No, no, no,' he answered, his eyes darkening and his mouth twitching. 'Everything is perfect.'

I looked away to the side, just in time to see Mr Squatsby grinning with delight – but only for a moment.

All of a sudden the Rats stood up. And the teachers stood up. And everyone stood up. Alone, in the silence, Petal walked slowly up the aisle, through the audience, to the stage. Her measured footsteps marked the seconds like the ticking of a grandfather clock. She looked at no one until she arrived on the stage then turned abruptly to face us. She raised a hand and lowered it. We sat.

'Thank you for coming,' she said, smiling a sweet smile which slowly faded. 'Dr and Mrs Crouchnail are gone,' she continued. 'They are gone and we are left to deal with their loss, to face the future alone. A future which we can face with worry and panic –' she raised her eyebrows, glanced towards the teachers – 'or with strength and courage. A problem we can solve. I –' her eyebrows slowly sank – 'am the solution.'

Silence.

'The school,' she said clearly, 'will continue to be run exactly as it was in the days of Dr and Mrs Crouchnail. Nothing has changed. Nothing will change.'

She looked out across her audience. Her audience stared back at her.

'Lessons will continue as they always have. You will go to them as you always have. You will behave as you always have. Those who cannot behave,' she said, 'will be dealt with as they always have been. Those who feel they cannot abide by the rules of the school will be –' she paused to lower her voice – 'removed. Nothing has changed. Nothing will change.

'And if anyone should ask you about this new … arrangement – your parents or guardians or relations or neighbours, for example – you will simply reply: "Nothing has changed." *Nothing.*'

Silence.

'Does anyone here feel that they cannot abide by this rule? Does anyone not understand what is expected of them?'

Silence.

'Good,' she said quietly. 'You may leave when told to do so.'

And with that she walked back down the aisle and out of the hall, her footsteps tick-tocking into the distance.

Eventually we all filed out of the hall in orderly, shocked silence.

I looked to Eg for his thoughts, but he had fallen into another of his dark silences.

'So,' I said, feeling like I should say something, 'what lesson have we got now?'

'Tell me again,' said Eg, jerking, as if waking up. 'Tell me again.'

'Tell you … what?' I asked.

'Tell me again how you came here,' he said, a tremor in his voice. He grabbed hold of my arm and began to shake.

'I don't …' I began. 'I don't know.'

'You do!' he cried. 'You told me before. Tell me again. Every detail. Remember everything!'

'Well,' I said. 'Like I told you before, I was in my bedroom. And then there was the stairs. I kind of … fell down them, through them. And then there was the tunnel and the door –'

'Yes, yes, and then? And then?' He was tugging at my arm, shaking me.

'Well,' I went on, trying to remember, 'at the end of the dark, I came up some stairs. And I banged my head. And I had to push through something. It was like a … like a blanket. And I remember the dust. I was in a room. And I came out of that room and I was here.'

Eg let go of me. The dark silence was gone. A light had arrived in his face. He smiled and grabbed hold of me.

'Come on,' he said.

'Where are we going?' I asked.

'Home.'

Chapter Ten
Under the Floor

'Come on,' said Eg.

The crowd were still filing out of Petal's assembly. He strode through and the people parted around him. I followed.

'What do you mean, *home*?' I called. 'It isn't time to go home yet. We've got afternoon lessons, haven't we? Where are we going?' But I knew what he meant. My fingers found the cold metal of the key in my pocket – the key to the door that had brought me here.

'This wasn't the plan,' I said desperately. 'I'm not going back. We're going to find the Crouchnails. I'm going to stay here with you, remember?'

'This way,' said Eg. He held a hand up above his head and waved. Soon we were joined by Eg's friends. Eric the Spud and Lulu, the tall, thin girl with the long dark hair, walking either side of Eg while I trailed along behind.

'All right, Eg?' said Eric.

'All right, Eric?' said Eg.

On we walked, Eg, Eric, Lulu and me.

But when I looked up they had gone.

A hand grabbed me from behind and pulled me into a doorway.

'Shh,' said Eg. We went inside, all four of us.

'What happened to the plan?' I asked as we marched along a corridor.

'This *is* the plan,' said Eg.

'Haven't we got a lesson now?'

Eg nodded. 'But we're not going to it,' he said.

I stopped and frowned. I called after them.

'But Petal said if we don't go to lessons –'

'Her name,' said Eg with a flick of his eyebrows, 'is JackGirl. Come on.'

We climbed some stairs and headed down another grey corridor.

'Why have you started calling her JackGirl?' I asked. Cold fingers of doubt were beginning to grab at my insides.

'First rule of battle,' said Eg. 'Know your enemy.'

We climbed another set of stairs. They were taller and steeper, narrower and cramped, winding up in darkness to a short, shadowed corridor. There were two doors, one to the left, one to the right and at the far end was another set of stairs going back down. We paused.

'Eric,' said Eg. His Spud friend nodded. 'I want you to wait here, at this end of the corridor. Lulu, I want you to wait at the other end, down there. Now, at the first sign of anyone coming up the stairs – anyone at all – you whistle. Really loudly. Understand?' Lulu nodded.

'What do I whistle?' asked Eric.

'You do requests?' Eg smiled. 'Do you know the tune to "Get Out Quick There's Someone Coming"?'

'No,' said Eric.

'Well, make it up,' said Eg, his temper slipping. 'It's only got one note and it's really loud. Can you whistle that?'

Eric nodded.

'I don't care who it is,' said Eg. 'A teacher, Gritts, JackGirl, a Rat, a first year, a Bullet –'

'A Bullet?' Eric looked confused.

'It's what he calls the girls who look like Petal – I mean JackGirl,' I explained. 'The ones with their hair piled up like a bullet.'

Eric laughed.

'Whoever it is,' said Eg, 'you whistle first and then you stop them. Have a fight, have a fit, start kissing, tackle them to the ground – whatever. Just stop them getting anywhere near this door.'

Eg was pointing at one of the two doors in the corridor. On it was a brass plate, and on that were engraved the words:

Dr and Mrs Crouchnail
HEADTEACHERS
Please knock then wait.

Eg knocked and waited.

I looked desperately to Eric then to Lulu. They smiled and shrugged.

Eg knocked again.

No answer.

Eg turned the handle and opened the door.

'The second rule of battle,' said Eg, 'is knowing when to retreat.'

And in we walked.

At opposite sides of the office were two desks, each with a tall leather chair behind it. Around the walls, hundreds of files and folders filled the shelves from floor to ceiling. And there was something about the smell of that office. Something I couldn't quite recognise.

'Look,' said Eg, 'another door.' On the far wall of the office, behind the desk, was a very old-looking brown door, carved in four panels, with a large brass handle and keyhole. 'I wonder …' murmured Eg. He tried the handle but the door was locked. 'Perhaps this is where the money is … or was … Or perhaps that's just another story –'

'What are we doing here?' I interrupted, needles of anxiety picking at my skin.

'A good question.' Eg smiled, turning his bright, blue eyes on me. 'A very good question. Now, remind me. Tell me again how you came to be here.'

'Again?' I said.

'Again,' said Eg.

'Well,' I began. 'Like I told you, I was in my bedroom. And then I fell through the stairs. And I came along the tunnel and through the door. And then I came up some different stairs and I banged my head at the top –'

'So,' cried Eg, walking around the room. 'If you banged your head on it, we can say with some certainty that the door through which you arrived was –' he stopped and looked down – 'a door in the floor. A trap door. And where might there be a trap door in this school that no one would notice, no one would find by accident. In a classroom? Unlikely. In a corridor? Doubtful. In the staff room? Possible. In the headteachers' office?' His eyebrows lifted then he looked at me. 'Go on,' he said impatiently.

'Well,' I went on, 'when I banged my head, I pushed up through something like a blanket –'

'So the trap door is covered with something, hidden by something. A blanket? Not very decorative to leave a blanket lying around on the floor. And a carpet would be difficult to get past. So perhaps a rug? And where are the only two places in the school where there would be a rug on the floor? Either the staff room – did you see a rug there when we spied through the hole in Gritts' cupboard? No, neither did I – or the headteachers' office. And so …' Eg bent down, picked up the corner of the darkly stained rug on which we were standing, flicked it to one side and smiled broadly.

There, cut into the floor boards, was a square of dusty wood with a metal ring set into it.

I looked at him. He looked at me. He smiled.

'It seems to be a trap door,' said Eg.

At which point there was a loud whistling noise from outside.

I looked at Eg. He put a finger to his lips, smiled and pulled open the trap door to reveal wooden stairs that disappeared down into darkness.

'I don't mean to be rude,' said Eg, 'but Eric – I think it was Eric – has whistled. There's someone coming. And we are here, uninvited, in the middle of the headteachers' office next to a secret trap door. Which is open. I think we should get in and hide, don't you?'

I put a foot on the top step.

Eg did the same.

I took another step.

Eg followed.

Another step.

Eg too.

Side by side, we climbed down the stairs until Eg reached up and pulled the trap door over our heads, stuck out a hand to tug the rug straight then let the trap door fall gently shut.

'I can't hear a thing,' I whispered. 'Is anyone up there?' A pair of fingers scurried across my face and pinched my lips shut.

'Can't you whisper quietly?' whispered Eg so quietly it might have been the sound of dust falling through the air.

I didn't whisper anything else for a long time. It felt like ten minutes, but it might have been less.

Eg's face appeared in a beam of torchlight.

'We could be here for ages,' said Eg. 'You might as well go now – as long as you go very quietly. Here you are.' He handed me the torch. 'You can keep it.'

'Go?' I replied. 'Go where?'

'Down the stairs,' said Eg. 'Home.' His mouth pinched into a thin line, almost as though he felt sad. 'This is what we came looking for, isn't it? The way home?'

'Home,' I said. I found my hand in my pocket, and, in it, the key I had been carrying since the day I'd arrived in this strange school.

I looked down into the darkness of the stairs that led home. I looked up at the darkness of the trap door. There was no need to choose.

'I don't want to go home,' I said. 'Why would I want to go home? I told you before. I want to stay here.'

'Are you sure?' he asked.

I nodded firmly.

'No matter what happens?' he asked.

'What's the worst that can happen?' I said carelessly.

'She'll kill someone,' said Eg, his smile dropping. 'Oh, she might not do it on purpose. She might not even do it herself. But if JackGirl's power grows, if she continues to play this game and win, then someone will die. Unless we can stop her.'

I nodded firmly again.

'Good.' Eg smiled, giving a single nod. 'I'm glad.'

We sat in comfortable silence for a little longer.

'How do we know,' I whispered as quietly as I could, 'when the coast is clear, when we can get back out?'

Silence.

I could hear Eg breathing.

'That,' he finally said, 'I have just realised is a tiny detail we forgot to arrange.' A snort of laughter bubbled gently beneath his whisper

I wanted to laugh. But it wasn't the fear and the silence and the darkness that stopped me.

It was the sound. The single, quiet sound above our heads: the door of the office being opened.

I felt Eg's breath on my face.

A quiet click. The same door closing.

The creak of a floorboard. Then another. And another.

Footsteps.

They were coming towards us.

Chapter Eleven
Toilets

The floorboards creaked. The footsteps were coming closer. And then they stopped.

'They're standing still,' whispered Eg. 'Or they're on the rug. Right above us.'

'*They?*' I froze in horror.

I sensed Eg shifting slightly, as though clenching, ready to spring.

I, meanwhile, was sitting with my head clamped helplessly between my knees. And that, I realised, was the difference between us.

I heard a voice above us.

'Eg?' it sounded like it was saying. 'Eg, are you in here?'

I turned to Eg. I think he may have turned to me, but it was hard to tell in the darkness.

There was a clatter of feet, a thump and a blaze of light that blinded me for a moment. I opened my eyes.

Eg was standing up, his top half poking out of the trap door. Staring down at us open-mouthed in the headteachers' office was Eric.

'What are you doing?' screamed Eric, his fleshy mouth flapping loosely up and down. 'You nearly scared me to death.'

'And how do you think we felt?' I screamed back. 'We're sitting down there in the dark while you prowl around like a … like a …'

'Who was it outside?' asked Eg. 'Why did you whistle?'

'Gritts,' said Eric. 'Came up the stairs with a bin bag, asked us what we were doing. Lulu told him that JackGirl had told us to wait there for her.'

'So JackGirl does have her uses after all,' said Eg. 'What did Gritts say?'

'Something about going to hell in a handcart and then he went on his way. So Lulu stayed outside on lookout and I came looking for you.'

Eg helped me up and put the trap door and the rug back in place. 'Clearly we need an all-clear signal before we do something like this again.'

'I won't be doing something like this again,' I said.

But I was wrong.

That night I watched the television again at Eg's house. I sat between an orange stain and a collection of plates welded to each other with something grey. I watched the same programme about the same people shouting at each other – or they might have been different people shouting about the same thing. I wasn't sure. Then I watched the News. It was still bad and scary. I turned it off and went to find Eg in his spotlessly tidy study.

I said hello.

'Mmm,' he said to himself. He was staring at a huge piece of paper covered in boxes and lines and scribbles.

I said hello again. He looked up.

'Ah, *there* you are,' he said as if he had been searching for me for days. 'Come and look at this map. The best place is here, I think.' He pointed at his huge sheet of paper.

'Oh.' I leaned forward to look.

'In the toilets,' said Eg as if making himself quite clear.

'What?'

'The best place to hide,' he explained.

'Hide?'

'Yes, hide,' he repeated.

'Eg, what are you talking about?'

'We need somewhere to hide,' he said.

'Who from?'

'Well, Gritts, of course. What do you think he would say if he found us wandering around the school in the middle of the night?'

'In the middle of the night?'

'Yes,' he said. 'When else can we have a good look around the headteachers' office without worrying about getting caught?'

'You're telling me,' I began nervously, 'that we're going to hide in the school toilets –'

'Yes, at the end of school tomorrow.'

'And then, in the middle of the night, we're going to go and have another look at that room with the trap door?'

'Yes,' said Eg.

And that was the end of that discussion.

The next morning I found Eg getting ready for school in his study.

'Right,' he said, casting an eye over a heap of stuff piled up on his desk. 'Torch, rope, bicycle chain, banana, candle, matches … and a few other things that might come in useful, I expect.' And with that he fed them one by one into his pockets until they were gone.

'Why do we need all this stuff?' I asked. 'And what's the banana for?'

Eg looked at me. 'Have you ever hidden in a toilet?'

I shook my head.

He smiled. 'You never know what will come in useful when you hide in a toilet.'

'And you're sure this is a good idea?' I said.

'If we want to find out what has happened to the Crouchnails, get them back and get rid of JackGirl,' said Eg, 'it's the only idea.'

And so we left for school.

JackGirl was right when she said nothing would change now she was running the school: nothing *had* really changed. There was still no sign of Miss Tremmel after her 'accident'. And two Spiders had not been seen since JackGirl sent for them. There was a fight outside the hall, which was soon stopped by a group of Rats armed with rounders bats and table legs. But, other than that, nothing unusual happened. Groups of Rats still roamed the corridors; we went to lessons; JackGirl sat on her throne in the art room and paraded through the school grounds on her chair at lunchtime; we ate lunch and went to more lessons. The only real difference was that everyone seemed a bit quieter than they had been.

'Fear,' said Eg. 'I can smell it in the air.' He took a deep breath through flaring nostrils.

The only fear I could smell was mine. It got bigger and smellier as the day went on until the final bell of the day rang and the time had come.

Everyone else went home. Eg and I went to the toilet.

I had been in those toilets before. But not with the idea of spending the night in them. There were white tiles on the walls, some cracked and stained, others missing altogether with something crumbling and blue in their place. There were three sinks and a small window above, its cloudy glass letting in darkish daylight. There was a tin trough with something like pond weed growing in streaks along it. In a corner, there was a small wooden cubicle that looked like it had been left out in a storm.

This cubicle, Eg said, was where we would hide.

We went in.

I put down the toilet lid and sat down. Eg stood by the door – mainly because there wasn't much room to stand anywhere else – and locked it.

'Time to practise the emergency procedure,' said Eg. 'If Gritts comes in, this is what we do. You stay sitting but pull your legs up so he can't see them under the door. Sit as far forward as you can. That's better. Now I go behind –' he leapt up behind me, crouching in what must have been an impossibly small space – 'and we wait for him to go out again. OK?' I nodded then he jumped down.

And so we waited.

And we waited.

The light through the little window began to fail.

And we waited.

'Eg?' I whispered.

'Mmm?' he said distractedly. He had been thinking again.

'You know when I first got here …'

'Ye-e-es,' said Eg.

'You know, that first day, when I was standing around outside and you came up to me and you said –'

'You're new, aren't you?' he interrupted, smiling at the memory.

I nodded.

'Why did you?' I asked. 'Why did you come and speak to me?'

Eg shrugged.

'Sometimes,' he said, 'sometimes you just know when something interesting is about to happen. And I wanted to find out what it was.'

I smiled.

'I'm glad you did,' I said.

Eg rummaged in his pockets and pulled something out.

'Fancy half a banana?' he asked.

'I wondered what that was for,' I said.

We ate the banana in silence.

And then we sat for a bit longer until the light had gone and we were in darkness.

'Do you think Gritts will come in here?' I said.

'Yes, he does his rounds every night before locking up. It was around eight o'clock last night,' said Eg.

'How do you know?' I asked.

'Do you think I was sitting around doing nothing while you were watching telly last night?' Eg smiled. 'I came up and stood at the school gates and followed the beam of his torch as he wandered around the school.'

'You didn't tell me you were going out,' I said, feeling left out.

'No,' said Eg.

The toilet seat was getting colder and harder. I stood up. Eg too was beginning to fidget.

'Time for a walk,' he announced. He went out of the cubicle and walked round and round the little dark room in a small circle.

'Ah,' sighed Eg, 'there's nothing like a good walk after sitting in a toilet cubicle for three and a half hours.' He paused at the sinks. He seemed to be examining them quite closely.

I was feeling quite bored too – but not bored enough to look at sinks. I watched him from the doorway of the cubicle.

Eg froze. He seemed to be listening to something.

Then I heard it too. Someone was walking along the corridor towards us.

I froze.

The door opened a crack and the beam of a torch shone in. Gritts' chewed-toffee nose poked after it.

I edged silently back into the cubicle, expecting Eg to follow. But he didn't. I eased the cubicle door shut, pulled up my feet and listened to the thumping of blood in my ears.

Beneath the door, I could see the torch beam moving. I heard footsteps, a scraping noise and a clanking thump. Then the torchlight went away and there was the sound of a key turning in a lock. Footsteps disappeared into the distance.

I waited in the silence, holding my breath until the ringing of my blood stopped.

'Eg?' I whispered.

Silence.

I came out of the cubicle but it was dark and Eg had the torch.

'Eg?' I whispered again, a little louder this time.

I went to the door to see if he was in the corridor. The door was locked. I stood very still and listened.

With my heart starting to beat louder than ever, I realised I was alone.

Eg had gone.

Chapter Twelve
Found

In the dripping cold still silence of the toilets, I could hear my breathing. It was getting faster. I walked from one wall to another, from the sinks to the cubicle, from the cubicle to the sinks. I walked from the sinks to the tin trough, from the tin trough to the sinks and back to the cubicle. I tried the door to the outside world again, wondering if I had made a mistake the first two times I had tried it. I hadn't.

Locked.

It was dark and I could see nothing. But one thing was obvious. I was locked in the school toilets. And Eg was gone.

I went and sat on the toilet in the cubicle again.

I remember thinking: *I will sit in here alone all night. I will be found in here by Gritts in the morning. He'll ask me how I got here. And then he'll kill me. Or worse, he'll take me to JackGirl.*

Then I started wondering if Gritts had already got Eg: whether he'd taken him to his cleaning cupboard and locked him in while he got help or called the police or –

And that was when I heard a noise. A tapping noise.

I sat perfectly still and listened.

Nothing.

I returned to my thoughts, in which Eg was tied up in Gritts' cleaning cupboard while Gritts hit him with a mop.

But there was that noise again. A kind of knocking.

I walked out of the cubicle to investigate. I walked all around the toilets, feeling my way in the darkness, walking and listening, walking and listening.

Nothing.

Then there it was again. I looked up at the ceiling.

It happened again. Tap, tap. From the corner of my eye I thought I saw a shadow pass across the grimy light at the window.

I went to the window and opened it.

I looked out but couldn't see anything – just the moon and some stars.

I looked down. I remember thinking how far away the ground seemed – about five metres. And then I noticed eight fingertips, clinging on to the windowsill.

'Hello,' said Eg. I peered down into the darkness. I could see his teeth. At first I thought they were smiling, but I think they were probably bared and grinding as he clung on.

'I wonder if you could help me in,' said Eg, puffing. 'It appears that after I opened the window and climbed out –' he paused and puffed a bit more – 'Mr Gritts closed it again.'

There was a low groan and the noise of skin scraping against concrete. Where there had been eight fingertips, there were now only four.

'Hold your arm down to me,' said Eg.

I did and his free arm grabbed it.

'Pull me up,' squeaked Eg, his voice grating against the strain.

I did and, after some heaving and grunting, managed to pull him through the window.

'You never really appreciate a toilet floor until you're standing on it,' said Eg, stamping his feet one after the other. 'Dangling in mid-air is OK, but I prefer it in here.'

'How did you end up out there?' I asked.

'Got caught out,' said Eg. 'In the wrong place at the wrong time.'

'But why didn't you come back to the cubicle like we planned?'

'Gritts would have seen me – or at least heard me. So while he was barging his way in, I opened the window and slipped out. I hadn't bargained on Gritts noticing it was open and shutting it. Nice to know he's so careful in his work,' he said, smiling.

'I thought you'd gone.' I looked at Eg with relief. 'I thought he'd taken you away.'

'Me? Get caught? Don't be silly. Right,' he went on before I could say anything else, 'I think Gritts should have finished his rounds and be off the premises in about ten minutes. Just time to open the door.'

'It's locked,' I said. 'Gritts locked it.'

'I thought he would,' said Eg. He rummaged in his pockets and pulled out a piece of wire. For a minute or so he poked and rattled it in the lock.

'Done!' Eg silently opened the door and closed it again.

'Wait a minute,' I said. 'If you can open any lock with that bit of wire, why are we hiding in the toilets? Why didn't we just come to school in the middle of the night and let ourselves in?'

'The front door's got a mortice cylinder triple lock on it,' said Eg, 'and the back door's bolted from the inside. Right,' he added, 'time for a quick sit down while we wait.'

He headed back to the cubicle and perched on the toilet.

About ten minutes later, we edged open the door to the toilets and stepped out into the darkness of the school.

As we creeped down echoing corridors following the beam of Eg's torch, every noise made Eg pause and me jump to a standstill.

A muffled clanking.

'The heating pipes cooling,' said Eg.

A scream.

'An owl,' said Eg.

Footsteps.

We froze and listened. Silence. We walked on, but there it was again, the tapping of distant feet.

We froze and listened. Silence. Eg took a step forward and listened. He laughed.

'Footsteps.' He nodded. 'Our footsteps. An echo.'

On we went, along the corridors and up the steep, narrow stairs that led to the headteachers' office. Eg shone his torch on its gleaming brass plate. It was strange, but now that we had arrived I felt safer.

The door was locked. Once again Eg fitted his piece of wire into the lock and, with a click, we were in. The faint blue light of night shone from the tall windows, across the office, across the desks and the rug to the old, four-panelled brown door on the far side. And again there was that smell that I couldn't quite name.

'What are we looking for?' I asked.

'I'll tell you when we've found it,' said Eg.

'Very helpful,' I said.

Eg laughed.

'Ah, a diary.' He opened a book on one of the desks and turned the pages, 'Meetings, appointments, events … Nothing significant, but they had several things arranged for this week and next week so they clearly weren't planning on disappearing.' He began to read aloud: '*Monday, 10.30 a.m., Petal.*' He paused and looked up. 'Interesting. Monday. That's the day they disappeared.'

He began to shuffle through the rest of the papers on the desk and hunting through its drawers. He even climbed underneath in case something was hidden there.

'Found anything?' I asked.

'Nothing,' he replied, shaking his head and wrinkling his nose. He lit a candle from his pocket and carefully perched it on the other desk. He gave me the torch. I looked through the files and folders on the shelves. There were files on which were written the names of every student in the school – I recognised some of them. I saw Eric's and Lulu's and even Petal's (which seemed rather fatter than most). And I'd just found Eg's file and was about to open it when he said, 'Right. Let's see what's behind that door.'

He stood looking at the old brown door on the far side of the office. He stared at the brass handle and keyhole as if he could open the door just by thinking – which wouldn't have surprised me.

He got down on his knees, inserted his piece of wire into the lock and turned it. He stopped. He removed the piece of wire, bent it slightly, put it back in the lock and turned it again.

'Something wrong?' I asked.

'It won't open,' he said.

'Why?'

'Because we haven't got the key and I'm using a bit of bent coat hanger to try and open it,' he said. 'It's an unusual lock,' he added, sighing to himself. He sat on the floor and stared at it again.

I'm not sure why – I think it might have been Eg saying the word 'key' – but I thought of the key I had in my pocket, the one I had found in the garden at home.

'I've got a key,' I said. I put it in the keyhole and turned it. With a satisfying click, it turned all the way round twice. I opened the door.

Eg sat and stared up at me. I could see his eyes glinting in the torchlight – and his mouth twitching as he thought to himself.

'Are we going in?' I asked.

Silently Eg stood up and pushed the door open. He shone the torch across dusty, worn floorboards until it reached a wall – the room was only two or three metres long. And that was when we saw it.

It was a small metal box in the middle of the floor, with a lid and a keyhole in which there was a key. But the lid was not shut; the box was too full. Eg stepped slowly forward as if creeping up to surprise it. With a shaking hand, he lifted the lid and shone his torch in.

Gold. Gold coins, gold rings, gold chains. All of them gold.

Neither of us spoke; we just stared.

Eg folded his arms, his eyebrows lowered in deep thought. And as he moved, the torch beam shifted.

'Eg,' I said. 'Look.'

He turned to follow the path of the light.

Lining the walls, stacked on wooden shelves from floor to ceiling, were hundreds of piles of paper. Small pieces, like sheets from a notepad, neatly laid out in piles ten or twelve centimetres high, each pile carefully spaced about ten or twelve centimetres from the pile next door.

'What are they?' I asked.

Eg stepped closer.

'Money,' he said. 'Piles of money. Piles and piles of money.'

Again we stood and stared.

Eg carefully picked up one of the piles, flicked through it then replaced it, nudging it back into place.

'Right,' he said. 'I think we can safely say one thing. Dr and Mrs Crouchnail haven't run off with all the school's money. And the theory that they've been arrested for armed robbery seems unlikely. People with boxes full of gold and shelves full of money in locked rooms don't tend to –' He paused. 'Unless that's how they got all this in the first place? Perhaps another look round outside, and then we'll go back to the toilets and wait for morning.' He yawned and opened the door back into the office.

As we came out, I became aware of a sound. A rattling. And voices. And the sound of a door opening. A click of a switch and light blazed full blast in the office. I blinked in the glare of it.

The office door was open. In the doorway three faces were staring at us, their mouths hanging wide.

Two of them were Rats. The other was JackGirl.

Chapter Thirteen
Trapped

Eg and me stared at JackGirl and the two Rats.

JackGirl and the two Rats stared at us.

I glanced at Eg. His mouth slowly closed into a smile.

JackGirl's did not.

'It's you,' she snarled as two more Rats pushed through the door and stood behind her.

'How very observant – it *is* us,' said Eg as another three Rats pushed their way in. 'What brings you here at this time of night?' he asked politely as a final Rat appeared, poking his head above the others to get a look.

'What brings me here?' growled JackGirl as the eight Rats formed a squabbling semi-circle behind her. 'I'm moving in,' she said, baring her teeth into something like a grin. 'Moving into my new office. What are *you* doing here?'

'Just looking,' said Eg, folding his arms.

'Looking?' snapped JackGirl, striding towards him. 'For what?'

'More of a who than a what,' said Eg. 'We were looking for Dr and Mrs Crouchnail.'

'I thought I'd made myself clear,' spat JackGirl through

clenched teeth, her bullet hair shaking with rage, 'they're gone. And they're not coming back.'

'Perhaps,' said Eg.

JackGirl narrowed her eyes for a moment as if wondering whether to thump him.

'Bunny? Ferret? Gormless?' she called over her shoulder. 'Don't just stand there. I can handle these two. Go and bring my stuff in.'

Three Rats disappeared and, with some puffing and squeaking and bumping and banging, two of them squeezed back through the door carrying JackGirl's throne. I noticed it now had a large fan of white feathers fixed to the top. The other Rat returned carrying a floor lamp with a tall pink shade.

'Put it down there,' she said, pointing. 'Plug the lamp in. And get rid of this desk. And the chair.'

Gormless and Ferret took one end of the desk each. Bunny picked up the chair. They heaved the furniture out of the door and an echoing clatter rang out like the sound of a heavy wooden desk and chair being tipped down some stairs. It was still clattering and ringing as the three Rats retook their places in the semi-circle.

JackGirl settled herself on her throne, her bullet hair surrounded by a halo of feathers.

'Mirror!' she called. One of the Rats approached, pulling a little round mirror from his pocket. She poked at her black eyes, eyebrows and hair, the golden bangles on her arm clinking and rattling.

'Does anyone know you're here? Doing this?' asked Eg. 'And, just out of interest, how did you get into the school?'

'Me?' JackGirl smiled, rising from her throne and marching towards Eg. 'I used my key.' She dangled a large bunch of keys under his nose, snatching them away before he could move.

'Does Gritts know you've got his keys?' asked Eg.

A cold silence fell in which JackGirl's eyes flared. She opened her mouth to speak.

And then she stopped. Her eyes narrowed and she said, 'That door's open.' She pointed at the door to the little room behind us. 'What's in there?' she asked, edging forward.

Eg took a step backwards. I copied.

'That door?' said Eg, nodding over his shoulder without taking his eyes off hers. He took another step backwards. I copied.

'Yes,' said JackGirl, taking a firm step forward. 'That door.'

'Nothing much,' said Eg, taking another step back and leaning against the door frame. 'Just papers,' he said, smiling and shrugging.

JackGirl nodded. She began to circle the office, prowling. Eg watched her, holding her gaze.

'Just papers?' she asked.

Eg nodded.

'Just bits of paper,' he said. 'Loads of them.'

She reached the door, reached us and, turning her cold black eyes from us, peered into the darkness.

'Bunny?' she called. One of the Rats stepped forward. 'Get me a torch.'

Bunny rummaged hurriedly in his coat pockets. One of the other Rats handed him a torch. He passed it to JackGirl.

She flicked the torch on and went into the little room.

We stood in silence, Eg and me, peering after her and listening to the sound of her footsteps and her breathing getting slower and heavier until they stopped altogether.

Eg followed her in and I followed Eg. I think a Rat, maybe Bunny, followed us.

As we entered she turned and the torch lit her face. Her eyes were burning blacker than ever and a genuine smile of joy – the first I had seen on that hard, pinched face – shone out at us.

And then the smile fell.

'How did you get in here?' she snapped. 'There's no key. It's always locked. How did you get in here? Give me the key. Give me the key now.'

Eg stood and said nothing. I stood and said nothing. Neither of us looked at the other.

'It's out there,' said Eg. 'In the desk. The one you threw down the stairs.'

She pushed past us and out the door, back into the office.

'Stay there, Bunny,' she called back to us. 'Don't let them touch anything.' She stopped and turned. 'Nobody… touches… anything.' A lingering glare, and she was gone.

Bunny settled himself in the doorway, arms folded, guarding us.

Eg looked left and right, lowered his head and charged. He barged Bunny the Rat out into the office, darted back into the little room and slammed the door shut. There was screaming. The door wasn't shut. An arm was trapped between door and doorframe, fingers snatching at us, grabbing at the dark air. I ran at it, smashing into the door trying to crush the life from Bunny's snaking arm. I opened the door again and began slamming it, slamming it until the arm was withdrawn and the door was shut and Eg locked it.

'Thank you,' said Eg, flicking the torch on and trying to breathe evenly.

'No trouble at all,' I said. 'I quite enjoyed it actually.'

A low, grinding voice from outside.

'I don't care,' it said, seething and spitting each word. 'I don't care how you do it. You get them out of there.'

'She seems annoyed,' said Eg.

'I think we'll stay here for a while, shall we?' I said.

'Possibly for the rest of our lives.' Eg smiled, sitting down on the floor.

There were other noises from outside. Bumping and shouting. A high-pitched whining noise.

'My arm,' it kept saying, 'my arm …'

And then silence.

Eg listened. I watched.

A rattling noise at the door. It stopped. Then started again.

'They're trying her keys in the lock. One by one,' whispered Eg.

He shone the torch around the little room, at the little box of golden treasure, at the shelves piled with money, at the ceiling, the walls, the corners.

'There must be another way out of here,' he said.

'Why must there?' I asked.

'Because if there isn't,' said Eg, 'and we don't want to spend the rest of our lives in here, we have to go out through that door. We will have to face a medium-sized gang of angry Rats, one with an arm you've just broken, and a surprisingly unpleasant girl who wants to kill us. Shall we start looking?'

We looked. But there was no other way out. No door, no window, no rug with a trap door beneath it: nothing but solid wall and ceiling.

'Listen,' said Eg sharply.

Silence.

'I can't hear anything,' I said.

'No,' said Eg. 'They've stopped trying the keys. They're waiting for us. Sitting and waiting. A siege.'

He began to pace up and down, up and down.

'Do you have to do that?' I said eventually.

No reply. He just paced. Up and down. Up and down.

I got up and wandered around the edge of the little room, shining the torch, looking for the way out that had to be there.

I stopped at the little tin box, shone the torch at the gold rings and coins and chains. I stooped and picked out a golden ring, turning it in my fingers, catching the torchlight in the diamonds that studded it and sent sparks around the walls.

'Do you think –' I began. 'Do you think anyone would notice if we … took just one thing?'

'Yes, I think they would,' said Eg. 'And I think they would call it theft.'

'It seems a shame,' I thought aloud.

'And what would we do with it, trapped in here?' Eg smiled. 'I don't see any shops. Do you?'

I replaced the ring carefully in the chest.

'We have a limited number of choices,' said Eg. 'We can open the door and give her the key. Or we can open the door and run. Either way, she gets the money. If she gets the money, she gets control of the money and control of the teachers and control of the school. Forever.'

Silence.

'And,' he went on, 'if we don't run fast enough, what will she do with us? Accept an apology and ask us to go home quietly?'

'I don't want to think about it,' I whispered, my voice suddenly hoarse. 'But I think it will hurt.'

'So there's only one thing we can do,' said Eg as if making his mind up. 'We're going to have to go back out there and somehow get ourselves down the trap door.'

'And then what?' I asked.

'That,' said Eg, 'is the one part of the plan which I haven't quite worked out yet. Take these.' He took four piles of money from the shelves and handed them to me.

'I thought we weren't allowed to take anything,' I said. 'I thought it was called theft.'

'We're not taking them,' he said. 'We're giving them to JackGirl. Have you got the key?'

I handed it to him.

'Follow me,' he said, 'and do exactly what I do. Are you ready?'

'No,' I replied.

He put the key in the lock and turned.

Chapter Fourteen
Out

Click.

The door is unlocked.

I picture JackGirl and the Rats out in the office. They have heard the key turn. Their eyes are on the door, their bodies tensed. They have started forward, ready to pounce on us.

Eg opens the door. And that is exactly what I see. Open mouths and grabbing hands lunging for us.

Eg is running. I run too.

Eg is throwing money, handfuls of money up into the air. I throw mine too.

And we stop as it flutters down on JackGirl and her Rats who slowly realise what is happening and dive to the ground. They scrabble on their knees to grab at the falling scraps of paper, to snatch up the money which scatters across the office.

Eg is on his knees, scrabbling among the others. With one hand, he lifts the rug from the floor, shielding us from the Rats and a shouting JackGirl –

'Leave the money! Leave the money! Get them! Grab them!' she shouts, flinging her pointing finger at us.

With the other hand, Eg opens the trap door, grabs me and pulls me down the stairs into darkness. The trap door bangs shut above our heads, and the rug (I picture it in my mind) floats back to the ground. Where we were, there now is no one. We are gone. Disappeared.

Stumbling and tripping down the stairs into the darkness, I realised Eg had stopped. In the shadowy half-light of the torch, he was on his knees at the top of the stairs.

Above us, the thundering of feet hammered and the sound of muffled shouting sent a cold weight falling from my neck to my feet.

Eg meanwhile was fiddling with a bicycle chain and padlock.

'What are you doing?' I said. I think I was shouting.

For a moment, he said nothing. With a final click, the padlock was shut.

'What am I doing?' he said. 'I'm running.'

And he was off down the stairs. I followed.

'What's the chain for?' I asked.

'I've attached the trap door to an iron ring in the stairs,' he puffed. 'It should slow them down.'

'I never noticed an iron ring in the stairs,' I said.

'No,' said Eg. 'But I have eyes,' he added, turning and smiling as we ran through the darkness. 'I noticed it the other day, when we spent some time sitting on the stairs. But the chain won't hold forever. The ring in the stairs is only fixed into the wood. And, if I'm not mistaken, I think I can hear the sound of splintering wood. Shall we run a little faster?'

We did.

But it wasn't long before the sound of running footsteps was following us, echoing through the black tunnel against the rhythm of our own feet.

On we ran, chasing the circle of light from Eg's torch into blackness.

'Stop turning round,' called Eg. 'Just run. You won't go any faster just because you can see them catching up.'

But I could see in the far, far distance behind us, round a bend in the tunnel, a light growing stronger: Bunny the Rat's torch.

'I don't remember the tunnel being this long,' I called.

'You don't remember much about this place, though, do you?' puffed Eg. I could hear him laughing, even as we ran.

'I remember that,' I said, slowing to a standstill and pointing ahead.

In the beam of Eg's torch was the door. The door where all this began. Its gold handle glinted in the torchlight.

'The key!' Eg was shouting. 'Where's the key!'

'You had it,' I shouted back. 'You opened the door upstairs, remember?'

'I put it in this pocket. With the bicycle chain and –'

He stopped.

'It must have fallen out when I pulled the chain out.'

Feverishly he emptied his pocket. The running footsteps were getting louder. The beam of a torch in the distance, coming nearer. And voices. Angry voices.

'Look again,' I said. 'Try the other pocket.'

His smile lit up the half-darkness. Pinched between two fingers, he held up the key.

'Teamwork!' he said, as he fiddled the key into the lock and turned.

On drummed the footsteps, nearer and nearer, closer and closer, and, as we opened the door, they appeared. Just metres behind us, running and shouting, JackGirl at the front, her teeth bared in the black hole of her snarling mouth, her bullet hair shaking, her bullet footsteps firing at us.

I stood frozen in a moment of terror.

Eg grabbed me and pulled me through the doorway. I turned and found him pushing the door shut, pushing and pushing as they pushed from the other side. I ran at the door and, with one almighty shove, it was closed. Eg turned the key and we were safe.

A thunder of kicks and punches shook the door, but it held firm. I fell to the floor, panting.

'Teamwork,' I mumbled into the dust.

A hand grabbed mine and pulled me upright.

'I think the door will hold,' said Eg, 'but we'll go on, shall we? Just in case?'

I staggered to my feet and limped on after Eg through the darkness.

'This is very interesting,' said Eg, when the sound of angry Rats had subsided. 'I've never been to another world before.'

I tried to feel pleased to be heading for home. But I couldn't. An old familiar nagging chewed at my stomach, sent lightning pains down to my toes.

And that was when we heard it.

Footsteps.

And a light.

I slowed down. I found myself walking behind Eg.

Someone was coming – not from behind but ahead. Someone was walking towards us. I could hear voices. A man's voice. And then a woman's voice, much louder.

I looked at Eg. He turned the torch off and we stood silent in the darkness. There was nowhere to go – other than back to the door and JackGirl and the Rats. And so we stood. And waited.

In the distance two silhouettes approached, bathed in a flood of light from a lantern. Ahead of them stretched the beam of a torch.

'I tell you, there's someone here,' said the woman. 'I heard them.'

'If you say so, my dear,' said the man. 'You're usually right about these things.'

'I can smell them,' said the woman, sniffing a long sniff.

The beam of the torch scoured left and right, ahead and around, until it found us.

Then a circle of light fell on Eg.

And a voice – the woman – said, 'Eg? What on earth are you doing here?'

'I was about to ask you the very same question, Mrs Crouchnail,' said Eg, his face alight with a smile. 'And Dr Crouchnail, too.' Eg stepped forward and offered his hand to the man. 'You have no idea how pleased we are to see you.'

'And who's that with you?' she said, shining the torch on my face. Her eyebrows rose and her mouth fell open. 'William? Is that you?'

'Hello, Mother,' I said. 'Hello, Father. I've come home.'

Chapter Fifteen
Home

Mother's frozen face thawed. Her jaw rose and her mouth closed.

'Where on earth have you been?' she growled. 'We were worried sick about you. Weren't we?' She turned to Father.

'Yes,' said Father quietly.

'We've been trapped in that house,' Mother went on, 'locked in like prisoners, and not a sign of you anywhere. How did you get down here?'

'I –' I began. 'There was a loose floorboard. I fell through a gap.'

'Nonsense!' she cried. 'Don't lie to me, William. Anything could have happened to you. What have you been doing?'

'I – I've been going to school,' I mumbled.

'School?' she screamed. 'What school?'

'Yours,' I said.

Silence.

I looked at Mother. I looked at Father. And slowly I understood – knew – accepted that I was also looking at Dr and Mrs Crouchnail.

And then came Mother's voice, her lips barely moving.

'How did you open the door?' she asked, every word falling like a cold stone.

'Door?' I said.

'The door, the door,' she cried, her voice rising, 'the one you have just walked through!'

'I found the key,' I said. 'In the garden. You must have … dropped it.'

Silence.

'You see,' I went on, 'what I think happened was that Dr and Mrs Crouchnail – I mean you, Mother – disappeared on Monday – which was because you'd lost the key. And I found it in the garden the next day. Didn't I, Eg?' Eg said nothing. 'And then on Wednesday I went to school and –'

Mother stared at me, her nostrils flaring wider with every quickening breath.

'Give me the key,' she whispered, 'and stop talking.'

Eg pulled the key out. I took it from him and held the key up to Mother.

Her bony, white, spider hand closed around mine, encasing it, squeezing it until I squeaked. When her fingers unfolded from mine, the key was gone.

'How is the college?' I heard Father asking Eg.

'Not good,' said Eg. 'There's been a …' He paused. 'Petal has … taken over.'

'What do you mean, *taken over*?' asked Father.

'You had disappeared,' said Eg. 'No one was in control of the school. It's chaos, Dr Crouchnail. Boys roaming the school, carrying out Petal's orders. She calls herself JackGirl now. Mrs Tremmel is in hospital, we think. Little by little, Petal has taken control. She's moved into your office.'

'I see,' said Father quietly. 'And where is she now?'

Eg smiled.

'On the other side of the door. Just down there.' Eg pointed back to the way we had come.

'I see,' said Father again.

'Don't just stand there mumbling, Crouchnail, you fool,' said Mother. 'Come *on*.'

Mother grabbed my hand, her fingertips sliding uncomfortably into the bruises she had pressed there a few moments earlier. Together we marched back towards the door. Eg and Father followed.

There were voices in the air when we reached the door. Mother put the key in the lock. The voices stopped. Mother turned the key and opened the door.

There stood JackGirl, surrounded by Rats sitting cross-legged on the floor. All heads, all eyes stared through the doorway at us.

In a flurry of scrabbling, the Rats got to their feet and ran, clattering down the tunnel into darkness. JackGirl stood alone.

'I hear that you have been terribly worried about us, Petal,' said Mother.

JackGirl's mouth hung open, her eyes flicking from me to Eg to Mother to Father and back again. Occasionally her lips twitched as though a question was trying to fight its way out – and failing.

'We're back now, though.' Mother smiled. 'So you needn't worry any more. That's nice, isn't it?'

JackGirl nodded. And with each nod her shoulders fell lower and her knees sagged and she seemed to grow a little smaller as though she were deflating.

'I've been thinking,' said Mother, taking JackGirl by the shoulders and turning her round, 'that perhaps you are not happy at our little school?'

Mother and JackGirl walked away down the tunnel, back towards the trap door, back to Dr and Mrs Crouchnail's College for Young Gentlemen and Ladies. And with each step the rigid frame of JackGirl sank until she was, once more, just Petal again.

'I wonder,' I heard Mother's voice say, as the circle of light in which they walked faded into the distance and Mother's arm tightened round Petal's sinking shoulders, 'I wonder if your parents would think that another school might be more suitable for you. I will speak to them. Immediately. I think that is for the best. Don't you?'

And with that they disappeared from sight.

Father looked at me, expressionless. His eyebrows performed a little jump before settling into motionless anger. I knew that face.

'You will go home now, William,' he said quietly, 'and you will go to your room until I call for you.'

Father turned to Eg.

'Eg,' he said, 'you will follow me back to the college. You will lock this door and return the key to me in my office.'

Father then turned on his heel and hurried after Mother. He did not look back.

We stood, Eg and me, watching until he was gone.

'So,' said Eg. 'finally we know who you are, William Crouchnail.' He smiled.

'You knew, didn't you?,' I asked. 'You knew. And I didn't. But you knew. You asked me that first day. I had to write my name on that school book and you looked at me in that way you do.'

'Well,' said Eg, shrugging modestly, 'I did notice something of a family resemblance. But you can never be sure, can you?'

I smiled at Eg. He smiled at me.

'I'd better go home,' I said.

'I'd better get back to school,' said Eg. He walked to the door, stood for a moment rattling the key in its lock, looking at his feet, at me, at the tunnel stretching ahead of him. He turned.

'Goodbye then, boy,' he said.

I smiled. I tried to speak, but nothing came out.

I took a long, deep breath. And there was that smell again, the smell I recognised in the headteachers' office and could not name: the smell that crept into every corner of school, every corner of home. It was soap – the blue soap that Mother washed me with every night.

'Do you think Mother and Father will let me come to school again, Eg?' I asked.

He smiled.

'That's the trouble with parents,' he said.

'One day, I'll come back,' I said. 'I'll come out of that house and live in the world again.'

'*Ne unquam respexeris*,' said Eg.

'Pardon?' I said.

'The school motto,' said Eg. '*Never look back. Only forward*. Mrs Crouchnail always says it.'

And that was when I knew what to do.

'Just stand there for a moment,' I said to Eg, pointing to a spot on the ground behind me. Eg looked at me, smiled and did as he was told.

'Goodbye, Mother,' I called from the door, my voice echoing down the tunnel and into the darkness. 'Goodbye, Father.'

I closed the door, turned the key in the lock and put the key in my pocket, patting it into place.

I turned to Eg.

'You coming?' I said.

'Where are we going?' asked Eg.

'Home.'

Chapter 16
The End

And so we walk down the dark tunnel, away from the door
– the dark brown door, carved in four panels, studded with
blackened nails, and its glinting gold handle – where I stood
all those days ago. It feels like weeks and years ago. Except
now Mother and Father are locked on the other side and I
am going home.

And where before, in the flickering light of my candle,
there were eyes and mouths in the blackened wood of
the tunnel walls and voices in the air, now there are just
wooden walls and torchlight and the voice of Eg.

And I feel scared and nervous and happy and worried
to be going home – which is the house where I lived with
Mother and Father before all this began, not Eg's house
where I've lived for the last few days. And I realise that
nowhere feels like home and I don't know where I want to
live and where I want to be.

As we walk, I look for the narrow brick corridor where I
came into the tunnel once upon a time, long, long ago. But I
don't find it. And I'm so busy looking, Eg is halfway up some
stairs before I even notice them. At the top of the stairs, we
come to a trap door. Eg goes first, opens it and climbs out.

I follow. We are in a small room with brooms and brushes and mops – a bit like Gritts' cleaning cupboard but smaller. There is a low, white door.

I open it.

We stand, Eg and me, blinking in the daylight of the hallway of my house. Behind us is the door to the cupboard under the stairs. I am not allowed in there. Mother says it's dangerous. I seem to have survived it. But I won't be going back in.

'What do you think they'll do – your mother and father – when they find we've locked them in school?' says Eg, blinking and squinting at the hallway in my house.

I pause and think about this.

'Mother will shout,' I say. 'And Father will look angry. Very angry.'

'But the school is connected to the house, obviously,' says Eg, looking up and down and around. 'They'll simply come out of school, walk around the hill and come in through the front door. And then they'll shout. And be angry.'

'Front door?' I reply. 'There is no front door. There is only one door – the door that goes out into the garden.'

I lead Eg through the hallway, through the Learning Room, to the kitchen and show him the garden door.

'Well, then they'll come to the front of the house and break a window and climb in,' says Eg.

'The only windows are on this side of the house,' I explain. 'They all look out on to the garden.' I point to the garden, to the brick wall that encircles it. 'There is no way in.

Or out.' And then I remember. 'There is *one* way. But I have the key.' I hold it in the air and smile. Eg smiles back.

'So that's why they built the tunnel,' he says. 'So they could get out – and keep you in.'

We walk into the garden and follow the line of the garden wall. Eg runs his fingers along its solid brick, his eyes climbing to the very top of the wall, higher and higher to the oval of grey sky above us.

'Too high to climb,' he mutters as we come to a little clump of green bushes.

'That's where I found the key,' I tell Eg, pointing to the bushes. 'And this,' I say, pointing, 'is the hole I was digging the day before I fell down the stairs and ended up with you.'

We look at the hole. It is nearly a metre across and over a metre deep now. We look at my spade – a birthday present from Mother and Father last year … or the year before. We look at the spade and the hole and the garden wall that rises up above it.

'They will get in, you know,' says Eg. 'It might take them some time to get under or over the wall. But your parents won't just leave us here. Have you got a ladder?'

I shrug. Eg explains to me what that is.

'No,' I say, 'I haven't got one of those.'

'And even if we had a ladder, where would we go?' says Eg. 'My house is the first place they'd look. And where else would we go?'

'I don't know,' I say. 'Where else is there?'

'Oh!' cries Eg. He pulls his hand out of his pocket and looks at it. 'Well, how did they get in there?' he says as though he's talking to himself.

He holds something up to the morning light. It is the golden ring I looked at in the money cupboard, its diamonds glinting, speckling Eg's face with brightness.

And in his other hand he's holding some pieces of paper. I recognise them: they are just like the pieces of paper we threw at JackGirl and the Rats. They are money.

'But –' I begin. 'You said that was theft!'

'It's theft if you take things on purpose,' said Eg. 'But not if they end up in your pockets by accident when you're under extreme pressure trying to escape from ruthless villains.' He smiles. 'And besides, I have a feeling these will come in useful where we're going.'

'Where *are* we going, Eg?' I ask

'Everywhere,' says Eg, his blue eyes burning.

I look at Eg. He looks at me. I climb down into the hole and begin to dig.

'We'll take turns,' I say.

He nods. His eyebrows are flickering. I know he is calculating how long it will take us to dig down, through and out of the other side.

'Eg?' I ask. 'Do you ever make mistakes?' He looks at me. 'I mean, are you always right?' He looks at me. 'I mean, do you always know what's going to happen next?'

'No,' he says, 'not always.'

The End

Going Underground

By Christopher Edge

For hundreds of years, people have dug tunnels beneath the ground. Some tunnels have been made by people mining in search of gold and silver. Other tunnels have been dug through mountains or beneath great cities to transport people from place to place.

Digging a tunnel is a dangerous business. Deadly gases can poison a tunneller or even cause a fatal explosion. Without warning, a tunnel can flood, or you could be hit by falling rocks and buried alive in a cave-in. Hundreds of metres below the ground, the chances of escape are slim.

In the following true story, you will read about how dozens of brave men in the midst of wartime risked even greater dangers to dig their way to freedom.

Prisoners of War

During the Second World War, captured British soldiers, sailors and airmen were held in prisoner-of-war (P.O.W.) camps. One of these P.O.W. camps was called Stalag Luft III. Located in woodland near the town of Sagan, a hundred miles south-east of Berlin, Germany, Stalag Luft III was designed to be impossible to escape from.

- The prisoners-of-war lived in barrack huts which were raised off the ground. This meant that the guards could easily spot any attempts to dig an escape tunnel.
- The camp was surrounded by a high perimeter fence topped with razor-sharp wire.
- Armed German soldiers kept watch from guard towers around the perimeter.
- Each guard tower was equipped with powerful searchlights.
- Anyone trying to escape the camp would be shot on sight.

However, these dangers didn't stop the captured prisoners from dreaming of freedom. They formed an escape committee to plan and organise any attempt to break out of the camp. Squadron Leader Roger Bushell was put in charge of this committee.

An ace pilot who had been captured after his plane was shot down, Bushell had already escaped from two other P.O.W. camps. After he was recaptured and sent to Stalag Luft III, he began to plan the most daring escape ever attempted.

Digging for victory

Bushell's plan was simple: they would tunnel their way out. However, instead of digging a single tunnel, Bushell decided to organise the digging of three separate tunnels. These tunnels were codenamed 'Tom', 'Dick' and 'Harry'. Through these tunnels, he planned to help over two hundred prisoners escape from the camp in a single night.

Work began on the tunnels. Other members of the escape committee faked identity papers and made everyday clothes out of blankets and uniforms so that the escaped prisoners could disguise themselves.

To avoid being spotted by the guards, the entrances to two of the tunnels were dug through the kitchen areas in Huts 104 and 123. These kitchen areas were built on top of concrete which was sunk directly into the ground, hiding the digging prisoners from sight. A stove was placed on top of one the tunnel entrances to hide it. Another was hidden beneath a camouflaged trapdoor. The third tunnel was dug in the washroom of Hut 122. Its entrance was hidden in a shower drain.

Down in the darkness

Between the prisoners and freedom lay many challenges. The German guards had buried microphones around the edges of the P.O.W. camp to detect the sounds of digging. The prisoners had to first dig a vertical shaft straight down for ten metres to make sure the digging couldn't be overheard. With no spades, they had to use make-shift tools made out of tin cans to dig with.

The P.O.W. camp was built on soft, sandy soil. Although this was easier to dig through, the freshly-dug tunnel could collapse at any moment, burying the diggers. To stop these cave-ins, they propped up the tunnel as they went using wooden boards from their bunk beds.

The narrow tunnels were barely wide enough for one person to fit through. In the cramped space, there was little air. To reach the cover of the forest beyond the barbed-wire fence, the prisoners had to tunnel for another hundred metres through the thick sand.

As they worked in six-hour shifts, the diggers faced constant danger of being discovered by the German guards. Every sound from the camp above could mean disaster.

A sandy problem

As the tunnels progressed, the prisoners faced a big problem: how to get rid of the sand they had dug out. Every metre of digging produced a ton of sand to dispose of. The prisoners couldn't just dump it on the ground around the camp because it was a different colour to the soil on the surface and would be spotted by the guards right away.

To get around this problem, they came up with a cunning plan. Hiding two bags of sand beneath their trousers, prisoners would walk over to the camp's garden area where they were allowed to grow vegetables. Whilst pretending to talk to the person gardening there, they would release the sand down their trouser legs. The gardener would then quickly cover it up with fresh soil.

Disaster strikes

By the summer of 1943, the German guards had become suspicious that an escape was being planned. They carried out surprise searches of the prisoners' huts and discovered the entrance to the tunnel codenamed 'Tom'. Thinking they had stopped the escape attempt, the guards blew the tunnel up. However, they didn't realise that two more tunnels – 'Dick' and 'Harry' – were still being dug.

Squadron Leader Bushell ordered his men to concentrate their efforts on completing the tunnel codenamed Harry. He was determined to make sure that his men could escape before the Germans had the chance to discover the remaining tunnels. By March 1944, their digging came to an end. They had dug beneath the barbed-wire fence – freedom was only metres away.

Digging without spades

To help dig the tunnels, the prisoners-of-war used:

- 1,200 knives
- 500 spoons
- 600 forks
- 4,000 bed boards
- 34 chairs
- 52 tables
- 600 feet of rope

The Great Escape

On the night of the 24th March, the great escape started. 200 prisoners gathered around the entrance to the tunnel in Hut 104. The men were disguised in everyday clothes with fake identity papers. One by one, they crawled down the escape tunnel.

As the first man came out of the tunnel, he made a terrible discovery. The tunnel hadn't reached the cover of the forest. The German guards, who patrolled the perimeter fence every few minutes, would be able to spot the escapees emerging from the tunnel.

Their nerves jangling as they waited for the coast to clear, the prisoners ran for cover one at a time. As the 77th man climbed free from the tunnel, he was spotted by a guard and a shot rang out. The escape had been discovered.

A terrible end

Raiding Hut 104, the German guards captured the prisoners still waiting to escape. A massive search of the surrounding area was ordered to capture the escaped prisoners.

The escapees had planned to catch night trains from the local railway station that would take them across Europe. However, in the darkness, many of the escaped prisoners couldn't find the entrance to the railway station. Within hours, many of them were recaptured.

Of the 76 prisoners who had escaped, only three made it safely back to England. Enraged by the escape attempt, Adolf Hitler, the German leader, ordered the execution of the captured prisoners. Fifty brave men were murdered in cold blood.

Today, a monument marks the entrance and exit to the tunnel that they dug – a permanent reminder of the fearless courage the prisoners showed as they tunnelled their way to freedom.

We would like to thank the following schools and students for all their help in developing and trialling *Eg and Me*.

Belper School, Derbyshire:

Wayne Bailey

Thomas Tween

Joseph Turner

Andrew Winfield

Sam Mart

Harry Everley

Izaak Devine

Holyhead School, Birmingham:

Ajay Sivia

Dashaun Ming-Stanford

Hassan Ibrahim

Ikram Hussain

Ayob Mahmood

Uwais Mahmood